INNOCENT
AGAIN

ISBN 979-8-9925708-0-9 (eBook)

ISBN 979-8-9925708-1-6 (print)

Book Cover and Interior Design by Damonza.

First edition 2025

Visit the author's website at www.stevendecker.com.

Published by TIER Books LLC

Author's Note

Innocent Again is my twelfth novel, and while it's my first legal thriller, I am blessed to be married to a career trial attorney. My wife Karen has served as a public defender, private defense attorney, and a prosecutor during her long and esteemed career. She reads every word I write in all my books. As a result, all of the legal matters that ended up in this novel were assiduously vetted by someone who is intimately familiar with the law and its practical application.

SD

INNOCENT AGAIN

A LEGAL THRILLER

STEVEN DECKER

NOVELS BY STEVEN DECKER

The Time Chain Series:

Time Chain
The Balance of Time
Addicted to Time
Time Travel's End

The Another Kind Saga:

Child of Another Kind
Earth of Another Kind
Gods of Another Kind
Genesis of Another Kind

The Second Chance Novels Series:

One More Life To Live
Walking Into Dreams
Shadow in Pursuit
Innocent Again

THE SECOND CHANCE NOVEL SERIES

Everyone dreams of getting a second chance—whether it's at love, success, or life itself. The *Second Chance Novel* series explores the transformative power of redemption and the human spirit's relentless drive to overcome adversity. While the classic "Second Chance at Love" trope is familiar, this series delves into deeper, more varied forms of renewal. Imagine a chance at a new life after one of bitterness and rejection, a disabled person striving to experience everything that the rest of us take for granted, an athlete reclaiming their competitive edge after a devastating injury, or a wrongfully imprisoned soul finally tasting freedom.

Each novel in the *Second Chance* series is a standalone story, offering a gripping journey through which characters rise from their darkest moments, fighting through adverse circumstances to experience triumphant highs. From heartbreak and betrayal to courage and ultimate victory, these tales will leave you cheering for the human spirit's boundless potential to persevere.

THE SECOND CHANCE NOVELS:

- **One More Life to Live:** An unexpected second chance at life, with a catch.
- **Walking Into Dreams:** A stirring second chance at love threatened by the power of the human mind itself.
- **Shadow in Pursuit:** A young man's courageous attempt to overcome a rival that has always defeated him—his best friend.
- **Innocent Again:** A woman is framed for murder. Three times.

PART 1

CHAPTER 1

May 28, 2004/Phoenix, Arizona

A S THE JUDGE turned to the jury, I was sure they'd find me not guilty. The sheriff's deputy would remove my ankle monitor, and I would walk out of there a free woman.

The judge's voice pierced the silent courtroom. "Has the jury reached a verdict?"

The jury foreperson stood. He was a middle-aged man, trim, with a gray beard, dressed in khakis and a polo shirt. I'd liked him from the start of the trial. He seemed to be an honorable man and had always looked at me with respect and hope in his eyes. "We have, your honor." His voice was neutral, and I couldn't draw any conclusion as to what the verdict would be from his tone or expression.

"Please hand the verdict form to the bailiff," ordered the judge.

The bailiff approached the jury box, and the

foreperson handed her the paper. The bailiff walked the document over to the bench and handed it up to the judge, who read the verdict to himself and then passed the paper to the clerk.

"Will the defendant please rise for the reading of the verdict," said the judge.

I hesitated, frozen in my seat. Rachel, my attorney, touched my elbow. I glanced at her, and she nodded, prompting me to stand. Rachel's fingers remained on my elbow as we stood together. My heart was beating fast. I couldn't believe my life had come to this after being so sheltered and comfortable. Until now.

The clerk read the verdict. "On count one, murder in the first degree: guilty."

That can't be right, I thought as my head dropped and my chin pressed against my throat. *I didn't do it!*

The judge addressed the jury. "Is this your true verdict?"

All twelve jurors nodded and mouthed the word, "Yes."

"Does either counsel wish to poll the jury?"

Rachel answered. "Yes, your honor."

The judge began the polling. "Juror number one, is this your true verdict?"

"Yes, your honor," said juror number one.

The judge continued, and all twelve jurors affirmed the guilty verdict.

"Thank you for serving on this jury," said the

judge. "The admonition barring you from discussing this case with anyone other than your fellow jurors is now lifted. You are free to leave. Thank you for your service. All rise."

The gallery rose. The jurors stood and left the courtroom.

"You may be seated," said the judge. Everyone in the courtroom sat. Rachel pulled me gently down into my seat. I was numb and confused.

The judge addressed the lawyers. "Are there any other matters before I set a sentencing date?"

"No, your honor," said the prosecutor.

"No, your honor," said Rachel.

The judge consulted with the clerk and then spoke. "It is ordered setting sentencing for July ninth at 8:30 a.m. in this division. A pre-sentence report shall be prepared and made available to counsel one week before sentencing. Sentencing memos are due at that time. Mrs. Moreland, I am now remanding you into the custody of the Maricopa County Sheriff's Office while you await your sentence. All bond is revoked. We are adjourned." The judge banged his gavel.

"All rise," said the bailiff. The gallery stood while the judge left the bench.

The sheriff's deputy, who had been present throughout the trial, approached the defendant's table, reaching for his handcuffs as he walked. "Please hold out your arms, wrists together, ma'am." His tone was gentle.

I turned to Rachel, who looked exhausted. There were dark rings under her brown eyes, and her black hair was disheveled. We'd become close during the past six months, and since my parents hadn't supported my claim of innocence, Rachel was all I had. She smiled weakly and nodded, indicating that I should comply with the deputy's request. I extended my arms, and the deputy snapped on the handcuffs.

"I'll try to visit you tonight," said Rachel. "But if they keep you overnight in the holding cell, we might have to wait until they move you to Estrella."

"What's Estrella?"

"It's the county jail for women. That's where you'll stay until sentencing."

"Okay."

"Remember all the things we talked about. Be strong."

I nodded as the deputy escorted me from the courtroom, my mind hazy with disbelief.

CHAPTER 2

THE SHERIFF'S DEPUTY led me out of the court-room and followed a narrow hallway that eventually reached the inmate elevator. We took the lift down to the basement and walked through a tunnel underneath the street into the jail. "If you'll step over to the metal detector, ma'am," he said.

I stepped through the metal detector, and no alarm went off.

The deputy led me to a room where three female officers were waiting. He stepped out and left me alone with them. One officer asked me to strip naked. I took a deep breath and forced myself to comply. I removed my heels, slipped out of the modest summer dress Rachel had suggested I wear for the return of verdict hearing, and then reluctantly slipped off my bra. I wondered if they would make me remove my panties, and the officer in front of me quickly clarified that with a nod and a hard stare. I removed the panties while she snapped on latex gloves. "Open your mouth," she said. I opened my mouth, and the officer swept a finger through my oral cavity. I didn't know for sure, but I suspected she might be looking for any pills or contraband that might have been in there. Next, she inspected my vagina and rectum. I cried softly, humiliated in a way I'd never experienced before. When the officer was done, she handed me a black-and-white striped uniform. "Put this on."

"May I put on my bra and panties first?" I asked.

The woman picked up the panties and bra and felt them with her gloved fingers. "These seem okay," she said. "No wire in the bra."

"Thank you," I said, slipping on my undergarments and then the starchy uniform.

One of the other female officers handed me a pair of plastic shower clogs. I put them on and an officer led me back to the room's door. I shuffled because of the loose fit of the clogs. The female officer gave me to the male officer, who had been waiting outside the room.

"Follow me," he said.

He escorted me to a cell. I looked at him. "Will I be transported to Estrella tonight?"

"Not likely. I think the last transport has already left."

The deputy opened the metal door to the cell. I entered the musty room and saw two other prisoners. The door shut with a clang behind me. I surveyed my surroundings as the deputy's steps echoed in the hallway and slowly faded away. The cell contained four concrete slab benches that emerged horizontally from the concrete wall. There were no mattresses on the slabs. A stainless steel toilet loomed in a corner.

I sat on an empty bench, as far from the other prisoners as I could manage. One woman sat directly across from me, while the other was catty-corner from her. They both wore the same uniform as I did, but I was sure they could tell I came from a different place in the outside world than them. The woman directly across from me was painfully thin, with stringy dark hair, a gaunt, pale face, and several missing teeth. One of her legs bounced relentlessly up and down in rhythm with her agitation. The other woman appeared stronger and more intimidating. Her brown skin and heavily muscled physique bore tattoos that ran down both arms and crept up from her uniform's neckline. Teardrop tattoos fell from the corner of one eye on her face. She glared at me with menacing brown eyes. "Rich bitch," she said.

I realized that even though I was wearing a jail uniform, my neatly styled, highlighted blonde hair projected an impression of wealth. I also understood, from a briefing with Rachel, that I shouldn't show any fear, so I stayed silent and maintained a stoic expression. This approach was clearly ineffective. The powerfully built woman stood and approached me. "You know what these teardrops say, bitch?" she asked, pointing at her own face.

"No, I don't," I said, forcing my voice to convey a lack of interest, adhering to Rachel's instructions on how to act when I was on the inside of a jail cell.

The woman smiled, then moved her arms fast and jerky, puffing out her chest and flashing signs. One arm swung up and out, the other down toward the floor, and her fingers spread into shapes I didn't recognize. "Dey mean I bean in da joint. You know, prison. Same place you goin.'"

I tried to take a stand. "Yeah, that's where I'm going."

The woman threw her head back. "Sheeet!"

The other woman shrieked like a hyena, laughing, but the gangbanger retreated, apparently rebuffed by my ruse of not being afraid of her. She sat back on her bench. I didn't consider it a victory. This was simply the beginning of a long nightmare. I wondered how I'd get through the night. Frankly, I was concerned about making it through the next five minutes. I'd had some self-defense training at the health club but had never really expected I might actually have to use it. Though terrified, I kept my stoic mask in place, determined to survive.

Following my December 2003 arrest for my husband's murder, authorities jailed me for a few hours before arraignment and determining my release conditions. The judge set bond at one million dollars. I paid a bail bondsman $100,000 (10% of the bond amount), surrendered my passport, and then they released me. While waiting for my trial to begin and during the trial, I'd been out on bond. While I'd had to wear an ankle monitor, I'd been free to live my life despite the emotional and physical toll of the trial preparation and the trial itself.

My conviction moved me from a six thousand square foot home in Paradise Valley to a ten-by-ten-foot cell that I was sharing with a drug addict and a gangbanger convict who, at that very moment, decided to start harassing me again. She stood and approached, jerking and flexing in front of me. I caught sight of a camera in the cell's corner near the ceiling.

"Cam'ra ain't saving your ass, bitch," hissed the gangbanger. "I cut your throat, and no guards hep you!" The woman waved her long fingers in front of my face as if casting a spell, weaving her hands around one another while her fingers writhed like snakes.

I pushed myself back against the wall as far as I could, refusing to cry, trying to summon the courage to defend myself if the gangbanger made good on her threat. Suddenly, the woman spun away from me and strutted over to the drug addict, sitting down beside her. The gangbanger whispered in her ear, and the skinny woman howled again with frenzied laughter.

Yes, it was going to be a long night.

CHAPTER 3

SURVIVED THE NIGHT in the county jail without being assaulted. The drug addict slipped further and further into withdrawals, writhing around and groaning. The gangbanger fell in and out of sleep, periodically rising and more or less repeating the same malicious acting out of finger-pointing laced with threats that she'd performed upon my arrival. My numbness to my cellmates' antics grew as the night went on, and by the time they moved us to the bus for transport to Estrella, I felt like a veteran. Making it through my first night of incarceration was a small victory, and it gave me a much-needed dose of confidence that I could figure things out and endure whatever was thrown at me while I waited for Rachel to file an appeal, win the appeal, and for the new trial to take its course.

A jury of my peers had convicted me of murder in the first degree. My husband, Peter Moreland, had died of a drug overdose, confirmed by an autopsy that detected a lethal amount of benzodiazepine in his blood. He had been drinking scotch the evening he died, and his glass contained ample traces of Xanax. I had a Xanax prescription, and the police found the bottle in our bathroom medicine cabinet. Empty. I was there on the night of the overdose; no one else had been in the house, and Peter had recently revealed to me he'd been having an affair with one of my closest friends. My fingerprints were on the scotch glass and bottle, although I don't drink scotch. The bottle of scotch was also loaded with benzodiazepine, meaning someone had tampered with the entire bottle. It wasn't me.

I told the police that Peter had seemed exhausted that night and had gone to bed early. When I woke up the following day, Peter was dead. I called 911. Peter had shown no signs of distress or anxiety during the evening of his death. He'd never sought counseling, worked out five days a week, and no one at his office had noticed any change in his behavior recently. In short, Peter had exhibited no tendency toward suicide. Everything fell into place for the jury to make a quick decision that I had murdered my husband beyond a reasonable doubt.

The bus ride to Estrella rattled my first-night survivor's confidence. What shook me was the extent of the precautions taken against escape. The bus was heavily fortified, with close-set steel bars on the windows and a barrier between the inmates and the driver. No one was getting to the driver. Three Detention Officers were stationed on the bus, as determined by the number of prisoners. We had handcuffs on our hands, shackles on our feet, and a belly chain around our waists. A long chain linked all of us to one another. If one inmate tried to bolt, she would likely trip over the chain, face plant, and topple some of the other inmates.

I gazed between the bars of the window and caught glimpses of people out on the street. I noticed a woman carrying three plastic grocery bags, accompanied by two children, around the ages of four and five, who watched expectantly for their city bus to arrive. Traffic stopped the transport bus, giving me time to observe them. Even though this was a poor part of town, I envied the trio standing at the bus stop. Their bus would eventually come. They would be on their way home. Meanwhile, I wasn't going home for a long time. Perhaps never.

Traffic cleared, and the inmate transport bus soon pulled into the sallyport at Estrella. We shuffled off slowly and were wanded by the officers working there. The procedure I'd endured the day before was repeated—strip, cavity search, new uniform, shower clogs, complemented by a thin rolled-up mattress, bedding, and hygiene kit. Next, they led me to my assigned housing unit, or as it was called at Estrella, dormitory.

My cell was on the first level of the unit. There were four beds in the room, three of them occupied. Each of the women lounging on the beds stared at me as I entered the room. One of them smiled openly at me. It was impossible to know the meaning of that smile, but I assumed that whatever the woman was thinking, it wouldn't be good. For me. I unrolled my mattress and threw it up onto the empty bunk.

"What you in for?" asked the smiling woman, a plump, brown-skinned person with close-cropped, dark hair.

"Murder," I said, trying to be nonchalant.

"Hmmm," said the woman.

I wanted to tell her I didn't do it, but rationalized that being known as a murderer might provide some level of protection unto itself. I remained silent. After making my bed, I turned back into the room to see what was going on. The short-haired woman was standing now, still smiling. "I'm Tanisha," she said. "Over there's Angie, and the lady on the bottom of your bunk is Blanca."

"I'm Becky."

"We gotta change that name, girl," said Tanisha, shaking her head. The others nodded.

"Why?"

"Too sweet. We call you Becks."

I thought about this and concurred that it was a good idea. "Okay. Becks it is."

Steven Decker

"You got money on your books, Becks?" asked
Angie, a white woman with a pock-marked face.

I remembered Rachel telling me what "books"
were—an inmate account for buying things at the
commissary. Rachel had also told me to make sure I
had someone on the outside who could put money on
my books. I had forgotten to do that. I hoped Rachel
would show up later to help me rectify the situation.
I sensed, however, that this was a weakness my cellmates were ready to exploit, so I hedged my answer.
"Sure. The money should arrive today."

All three of the other women erupted in laughter.

"What's so funny?" I asked.

"Nobody get dare books filled on Day One," said
Tanisha. "Gonna be a week a'fore you see duh money."

"Okay," I said. "I can wait."

"You can wait, but with no commissary, you got
nothing ta trade, honey."

"I don't need to trade," I said.

Angie smiled, nodding her head while the other
two chuckled.

"What am I missing?" I asked.

More laughter, laced with derision.

"You straight or what?" asked Tanisha. The other
two women laughed again.

"Straight," I said.

"We gone have to change that too. Less you got
commissary to trade."

CHAPTER 4

RACHEL CAME TO meet me in the afternoon. A
detention officer approached my cell. "Moreland," the D.O. announced, opening the door.
I sat up in my bunk, having spent the entire time there,
thinking I'd be safer from a higher vantage point. The
urge to urinate became more pressing now that an
opportunity to do so had finally arisen.

"I'm Moreland," I said, raising my hand.

"Privileged visit. Come on."

"What does that mean?" I asked.

"Your lawyer's here to see you," said the D.O. "Move
it!"

I climbed down from the bunk and approached
the door to the cell.

"Wrists out."

I extended my arms, and the guard snapped
on the cuffs. She escorted me into the hallway and
walked beside me as I shuffled in my clogs, trying to
keep up. We made our way out of the dormitory and
entered another hallway where the visitation rooms

were located. The guard led me into a private visitation room where Rachel was waiting. Rachel sat on one side of a table that was bolted to the floor. "Take a seat," she said. I sat in the other cheap plastic chair. The guard left and closed the door behind her. "How are you holding up?" she asked.

"I'm scared."

"I hear you. It gets better. What can I do to help?"

"I need to pee," I said.

Rachel lifted her eyebrows. "There's a toilet in the cell, right?"

"Yeah, but I'm afraid to use it. I need money on my books. The women in my cell are threatening to assault me sexually unless I trade something from the commissary for them leaving me alone."

"I'm sure I told you to arrange for that," said Rachel.

"I forgot, Rachel. There's a lot going on for me."

"Of course. First, let's take care of your immediate need."

Rachel called in a guard, who then escorted me to a nearby restroom. It was challenging to pull my pants down while cuffed, but I managed. When they returned me to the visitation room, Rachel was all business. "Do you have anyone in mind who can add money to your account?"

"Can you do it?" I asked.

"No, I can't. I'm your lawyer. It's not done that way. Is there someone you know who can do it?"

"What do they have to do?"

"The person can come to Estrella and put the money on the books. They'll take cash or checks. I imagine cash would be better since you're in a hurry."

I didn't understand why Rachel couldn't help me, but I accepted her answer because I trusted she would tell me the truth. "How much money should they bring?"

"I'm not sure what the limit is, but if your person brings a hundred dollars, that should be more than enough. The commissary doesn't sell a lot of stuff. It's candy, cigarettes, personal hygiene items, and things like that."

"That doesn't seem like enough money to buy my way out of trouble."

"It's a different economy in here," said Rachel. "The value of a pack of cigarettes is much more than it is on the outside, for example."

"Okay," I said. "I've thought of someone who might do it. Do you remember the guy who I pointed out in the courtroom gallery? The one who came to watch most of my trial?"

"Yes, your husband's business partner, right?"

"Yeah, Rick Miller. Could you contact him for me and ask him to bring a hundred dollars in cash down here?"

"I'll do that to help get you started," said Rachel. "After that, you'll need to call him from the inmate phone line, which is a recorded line, by the way."

"Why does it matter if the calls are recorded?" I asked. "I'm already convicted and locked up."

"It's just a way of life you need to get used to. Everything you say or do can be used against you to make your life in here worse."

"Okay, I understand," I said, still not fully grasping how they might use my words against me. "Can Rick visit me while he's here?"

"He can if he's on your visitation list. You just need to tell a D.O., and they'll let you know how to arrange that."

"All right," I said. "Do you need the number of Sleekfit Attire? I don't know Rick's home number, but I'm sure you can reach him at work." Sleekfit Attire was the company that Peter and Rick had owned together.

Rachel nodded. "Yes, that would be helpful."

I gave her the number, which I remembered well since I'd called Peter there dozens of times.

"Okay," she said. "It's getting late, and they'll be calling you to dinner soon, so we should wrap this up."

"Can you tell the warden or the judge I'm being threatened?"

"I'm sorry, Becky. The judge is not an option, and the warden isn't either. Threats are a way of life in here, and inmates have to figure out ways of getting around them if they can. If you are physically harmed, you can report it. But right now, you only have verbal threats. Hopefully, Rick Miller can get down here and fund your books immediately. I'll call him as soon as I get back to my office."

On my way back to the cell, I asked the guard how to add people to my visitation list. The guard took me to the place where they kept the forms. I filled out the visitation form, put Rick Miller's name on it, and submitted it. After that, the guard returned me to my cell. I noticed Tanisha was no longer there, and her mattress, bedding, and belongings were gone.

"Where's Tanisha?" I asked.

"She rolled up," said Blanca.

"What's that?"

Angie explained. "Rolled up mean she rolled up her mattress and took her shit. She's gone to Perryville to do her time."

"Oh, I see," I said. "Do you know how long her sentence is?"

"What's it to you, baby?" asked Angie. "You be doin' life for murder. Tanisha be out on the streets while you frying up there for years and years." My two remaining cellmates laughed, enjoying my misery, I guess. But I reflected on what Angie had said. Life in prison would be an unending nightmare for me—a perpetual cycle of hell on Earth.

The next day, a guard came and again took me to the inmate visitation area. This time, they took me to an open room where inmates sat in chairs and spoke by phone with their visitors, who sat across from them, separated by a thick glass wall. They led me to a numbered slot, sectioned off from other inmates by additional glass partitions. I sat and saw Rick Miller sitting across from me. He picked up the phone on his side, and I grabbed the phone on my side.

"Oh my goodness, Rick! Thank you so much for coming!"

"Sure," he said. "I put the hundred bucks into your account, so I figured I'd try to visit, too. I guess you put my name on a list or something."

"Yes, I did. Thank you for visiting! You have no idea how much having money on my books will help me in here. And what a great surprise that you're visiting!"

Rick was a handsome man in his early forties, with short dark hair and a clean-shaven, chiseled face. He wore a T-shirt and shorts, his usual work attire. Even though we were indoors, he was wearing the exotic Prada sunglasses he never seemed to be without. They had a sleekly curved lens that wrapped all the way across, covering both eyes, and a frame with open grooves in the arms, with the word "PRADA" engraved in them. He looked out of place there in the jail, but his demeanor was amiable. "I'm happy to help, Becky. You know I'd do anything I can for you."

I was so elated to see someone from my world that words just kept spouting out of my mouth. "I also never got to thank you for taking Rusty after I was incarcerated." Rusty was my Irish Setter.

"No problem," said Rick. "Katlin and I and the kids love dogs, and Rusty gets along fine with Buster."

"Thank you for coming to the trial," I said, trying to keep the conversation going.

"Oh, sure. I came as often as I could. I wanted to show my support. I'm so sorry for what happened, Becky. You must be devastated."

"Yeah, that about sums it up," I said. "Peter's gone, and now I'm being unfairly imprisoned for the rest of my life." I scolded myself after saying this because I remembered Rachel's warning about the phone conversations being recorded. But as I thought further about what I'd said, I figured my claim of innocence was probably quite common among the inmates here and would do me no harm if anyone ever listened to the recording.

"Are you going to appeal?" asked Rick.

"Absolutely."

Rick's next question surprised me. "Has any new evidence turned up that can help you?"

I paused, thinking. "I'm not sure. Do you know anything that might help me?"

Rick was quick to respond. "No, I'm sorry, Becky. But if I think of anything, I'll let you know."

I scrutinized Rick's expression during this exchange. What did I see in his eyes, partially hidden by his sunglasses? He was blinking rapidly and his gaze shifting from side to side. I didn't know what it meant, but I would have plenty of time to think about it later. Rick and his wife Katlin were close friends with Peter and me, and Rick had seemed nearly as devastated by Peter's death as I was. But now he seemed different. What was going on with him?

"Time's up!" said the D.O.

The end of the visitation had come too quickly. I needed to talk more with Rick and hastily came up with a way to get him to come back. "Can you bring another hundred next week?" I asked, not expecting to actually need the money. "I promise to pay you back," I said, giving him my most pleading smile.

The phone connection dropped, but Rick answered my question with a nod and a smile. He stood and gave me the thumbs-up sign. Knowing that spending a week in here was a long time, my smile faded, but I nodded back. Rick left, then a guard returned me to my cell.

CHAPTER 5

HAD TIME TO think about my conversation with Rick Miller that evening. With Tanisha gone and no one yet placed in her bunk, Angie and Blanca seemed disinclined to make any physical advances toward me. Their jaded attitude persisted, but they only verbally abused me, focusing on my privileged background and the suffering they predicted for me in prison. I was entirely in agreement with their prognosis.

As I lay there on the top bunk, I thought about Rick's eyes during our brief interaction surrounding his inquiry about "new evidence." I asked myself if I could use one word to describe his eyes at that moment, what would it be? I let my mind relax, closing my eyes and recreating the scene. The word came to me: *wary*. In a split second, right when I'd asked him if he knew anything that might help me, he'd gone from nonchalant to guarded. I wondered why.

Did Rick know something? Something he hadn't revealed when interviewed by the police after Peter's death? I knew Rachel had read the police reports, including their summary of the interview with Rick. He'd said that Peter had been acting completely normal at work and had plenty of friends and no enemies. So why was there wariness when I asked him if he knew anything that might help me?

Just then, the threads of an idea wove themselves together in my mind. I recalled Rachel's advice to be cautious about my phone conversations in the visitation room because they were all recorded. I wondered if she could access recordings of my conversations if they contained anything relevant to my case. I believed strongly that she could. If the phone calls contained meaningful information, Rachel should be able to get the tapes. I'd check that out with her the next time we met, but my focus now was on Rick. I would need to be careful about what I said and asked during our next meeting. But it didn't mean I had to be truthful.

Rick came to see me one afternoon, about a week after his first visit. I thanked him profusely for putting more money on my books and for spending a few minutes with me. During the past week on the inside, I'd been one of the best customers at the commissary and had been handing out snacks, candy, cigarettes, and shampoo like hotcakes, buying off people who threatened me. Rachel had cautioned me to be more discriminating about who I paid off because my overly gratuitous approach could backfire on me. My reputation as an easy mark might attract threats. Since then, I'd become more careful. If a person threatened me, I would check with the one or two people I trusted about the veracity of the threat, then decide whether to act on it. And even though my spending at the commissary had declined because of my more prudent approach, I was glad Rick had filled my coffers again.

"I owe you two hundred dollars," I said.

"Oh, don't worry about it," said Rick. "It's nothing." He raised the arm that wasn't holding the phone and pushed his hand toward me, emphasizing his assertion that the money didn't need to be repaid.

"No, I really need to pay you back," I insisted. "And I have to figure out a way to keep the flow of funds coming without inconveniencing you any more than I have already."

Rick seemed more than willing to continue helping me. "I'm happy to bring you the money once a week for as long as you need me to. The company's doing really well, and after all, the key man life insurance is buying all of Peter's stock for me, so now I'm making double what I *was* making. That life insurance money should have gone to you, not Peter's brother and sister."

The way the key man life insurance policy on Peter had been intended to work was for the money to go directly to me to buy out the fifty percent stake in the business I would have inherited from Peter. Rick would get the stock, and I would get the money. However, my conviction for Peter's murder meant that I was no longer entitled to the insurance proceeds. The life insurance payout would go to Peter's nearest relatives, in this case, his brother and sister. When the payout occurred, Rick would gain full company ownership, but Peter's brother and sister, not I, would receive the insurance money from Peter's stock purchase.

The insurance money wasn't critical for me, especially since it seemed I'd be spending my life in prison. And even though my parents weren't speaking with me now because they believed I had killed Peter, they'd taken care of me financially long before I even met my husband. I had a trust fund I could draw from whenever needed. But I rarely dipped into it while Peter was alive. The business he and Rick had built together, a women's clothing company with production in Asia, was highly lucrative. The inconvenience now was that I couldn't access my trust fund, at least in the short term. However, I had other ideas on how to use the trust fund. One was to gain Rick's trust in me. "I'd like to find a way to give you access to my trust fund," I said. "That way, you can just withdraw the money needed for my books here from there. I'm going to speak with my attorney about that and get her to draw up some papers to make that happen."

"It's not necessary, Becky," Rick said, waving his

hand back and forth. "I could give you a hundred bucks a week for the rest of your life and not even notice it. Plus, I enjoy seeing you. It's a real shame that your parents have disappeared from your life."

I ignored Rick's comment about my parents because I was running out of time. I'd long since forgotten about their emotional abandonment, supposedly because they believed I was guilty, but more likely because of their embarrassment at the country club at having a daughter who was a convicted murderer. What I needed to do now was to plant the seed I'd been growing in my mind. I leaned forward, lowering my voice. "Say, Rick, there's been a new development in my case."

Rick raised his eyebrows. "Oh really? Something good, I hope."

"Oh yeah," I said. "Really good."

I had Rick's full attention now. "Awesome!" he said, but his expression revealed masked concern. "Can you tell me what it is?" he asked. His tone was casual.

"Well, my attorney told me not to tell anyone, but since you're basically the only friend I have on the outside, and because I know you'll keep this absolutely confidential..." I paused, waiting for Rick to nod, which he did with enthusiasm. "They think someone else was in the house at the time of Peter's overdose."

Rick sat back in his chair. His smile evaporated into a frown, which he quickly erased, putting back on a rigid smile. "Great! What did they find that they missed the first time?"

"They found fingerprints!" I whispered.

His eyebrows went up again, but the forced smile remained on his face. "Where did they find them?"

"Uh, I'm not sure," I said. "But it was someplace they hadn't looked before."

"Do they know whose they are?"

"Not yet. But they're working on it."

"Could it be the housekeeper?"

"No, they said they weren't from the maids."

"Wow," he said. "I hope it leads to something good!"

I had never heard such false words, delivered in such a phony tone, in my life.

"Times up," said the D.O. The phone connection was cut.

I hadn't expected Rick to be so foolish as to reveal anything that might incriminate himself during his visit that afternoon, but as I thought about it, he'd already given me his motive. If Peter died, Rick's ownership position would go from 50% to 100%, and that's precisely what was happening. And while he'd given no verbal sign he was involved in Peter's death, his body language and facial expressions certainly had. Plus, I'd set the stage for follow-up questions during subsequent visits. I would devise a way to get him to say something incriminating so the recording would etch it into history. And it didn't take long for that to happen.

CHAPTER 6

ANOTHER WEEK WENT by, and Rick visited again. His Brooks Brothers suit, blue button-down shirt, and red paisley tie surprised me. "Whoa!" I said. "You're awfully fancy today."

"Yeah, I've got customers coming in this afternoon. They want to see next year's line-up in our showroom."

"And business is still strong?"

"Oh yeah. We're already nearly booked to full capacity for the fall orders. Probably will be after today's meeting."

"That's great, Rick! You're doing great."

"Thanks, Becky." Rick leaned forward. "And how about you? Any news on the stuff we talked about last week?"

"Yep. Big news."

Rick's eyes opened wide. "What?"

"They think it's a woman."

"Interesting." Rick's expression conveyed relief.

"Which is why I wanted to ask you if you knew Peter's girlfriend very well."

Rick scrunched up his lips. "Yeah, I knew Gabriella. She was a model at one of our photoshoots. I'm sorry that whole thing happened between her and Peter. But I know for a fact that he'd cut it off with her."

I nodded. "That's what he told me. I believed him. We both wanted to make our marriage work despite his little fling with Gabriella."

"Is Gabriella a suspect?" asked Rick.

"They're going to get her prints to see if they match the ones found at the house."

"I doubt whether it's her," said Rick.

"Why?"

"Because she wouldn't do it herself if she wanted revenge against Peter. No one with any sense would."

"What would they do?"

"They'd hire a hitman. Or, in this case, a hit *woman*, I guess. That's what I'd do."

"Hitmen are just in the movies, Rick. That stuff doesn't happen."

"Actually, it's really easy to find one. You can even find them on Craigslist if you know the right way to go about it. Uh, I mean, so I'm told."

"I didn't know that," I said.

"Time's up," said the D.O., and they cut the connection.

I had to endure nearly a week after the latest visit from Rick before Rachel came to see me. By that point, I had

been in Estrella for twenty days of the forty-two leading up to my sentencing hearing on July 9. I'd gotten
the hang of things in jail, and although most of my
fellow inmates resented me because of my background,
I kept most of them at bay with bribes from the commissary. It also helped that I was fluent in Spanish
from summers during my high school years spent on
church missions in Mexico. I was often called upon to
interpret during disputes between Spanish-only and
English-only speakers. However, my "success" in jail
life wasn't what I wanted to discuss with Rachel during
our privileged private meeting. I was eager to tell her
about what had transpired with Rick.

I told Rachel about each of my three meetings with
Rick. I explained how his wariness was apparent in the
first meeting, when I asked if he knew anything that
could help my appeal; how during the second meeting, he disclosed a motive; and in the third, that he
told me how he would execute the crime by hiring a
hitman if he wanted to kill Peter.

Rachel's first reaction was frustration. "Becky, how
many times have I told you not to speak about your
case without me being there? And to be especially
careful of what you say on a recorded phone line!"

"But Rachel, you're missing the point! We've got
him! All we have to do is get those phone recordings.
And let's face it, he would have clammed up if you'd
been there with me."

That explanation seemed to turn her thinking around. "Hmmm. What was the motive?"

"He doubled his ownership position and his income when Peter died."

Rachel nodded. "What exactly did he say?"

"It all started with the hundred dollars a week he's been putting on my books. When I offered to reimburse him, he waved me off and said he could give me a hundred dollars a week for the rest of my life and not even feel it, because he benefited from Peter dying."

"What else?"

"He said that nobody would be stupid enough to kill Peter themselves. They'd hire a hitman. When I said that only happens in the movies, he told me I was totally wrong. That you could hire a hitman on Craigslist! Then he backed off and clarified by saying that's what somebody told him. It was like he realized he'd said too much."

Rachel sat back in her chair. "Becky, that was admittedly a very odd way for Rick to speak about Peter's death, but it's far from a confession, and I'm sorry to say it wouldn't hold up in court."

When I heard this, my temper flared. "You're kidding me! He did it! I'm certain he did it!"

"But how, Becky? You were the only one there at the home when Peter died."

"That might not be true!" I said. "What if someone had been hiding there, waiting for the right moment?"

"I suppose that's plausible, but we need that on tape if we're going to make this thing stick."

I shook my head, frustrated, but my mind was whirling. "I just don't know how I can get a confession out of him. He's not that stupid."

Rachel wasn't so sure. "You'd be surprised what people say to others about crimes they've committed. Let me ask you a question. Would you say that Rick Miller has a big ego? I mean, he owns this wildly successful company. He's wealthy."

"Rick has one of the biggest egos ever," I said. "He was always bragging when the four of us would go to dinner. And Peter told me that Rick had confronted him a few times about their equal ownership position."

"Why did he do that?"

"He wanted a bigger piece of the ownership because he believed he was responsible for the company's rapid growth."

"Was that true?"

"I doubt it. Unless Rick was making a bunch of sales out on the golf course! He golfs twice weekly, gets into the office around ten, and is never there past three. I'm not saying Peter was a workaholic by any means, but he got to work by 8 a.m. every day and always worked until at least 4:30. Peter was in charge of product design, which is how the company made its mark."

"So it's safe to say that Rick thinks pretty highly of himself."

"Oh yes, definitely. Why?"

"Really arrogant people tend to think they're smarter than everyone else."

"That's Rick!"

"And because of that, they tend to be loose-lipped when they think they've outsmarted everyone. If Rick was responsible for Peter's death, he's still congratulating himself for planning the perfect crime. After all, you've been convicted; he was never even a suspect. I think you might have him right where you want him. I wouldn't be at all surprised if he comes close to confessing. And if he does, I'll make sure we get the tapes. Okay?"

"Yeah, fine. That's great. But how do I tease it out of him? Does it matter if I lie to get him to say something incriminating?"

"Not necessarily," said Rachel. "But I can't know for sure until I listen to the conversation, and we're a long way from that. One thing is certain. It depends more on what he says than what you say."

"Okay, I'll work on it. Can you come to see me next week?"

"Sure. Be careful, Becky. Okay?"

CHAPTER 7

THEY RETURNED ME to my cell, and I couldn't figure out how to get Rick to say more. But I wasn't giving up. I started thinking more deeply about my daily routine back home in Paradise Valley, specifically, where I'd been and what I'd been doing when Peter got home the day of his death. Peter always came home at five p.m., like clockwork. The first thing he'd do upon entering the house was to have a scotch on the rocks. I'd have his first drink ready for him. He'd grab the drink from the bar in the den, put on headphones, and listen to jazz. The soothing music and the scotch seemed to ease his nerves after a stressful day.

I rarely joined Peter in the den when he got home from work, even on days I wasn't working out. He preferred to decompress alone before spending time with me. I'd have a glass of white wine in the kitchen while he enjoyed two or three glasses of scotch. Three afternoons a week, I worked out in the gym we had set up in the pool house. On workout days, I'd prepare

Peter's first drink and leave it on the bar in the den. Then I'd walk through the kitchen, cross the pool area, and enter the pool house for my workout. On the day Peter died, it was a workout day. I'd fixed his drink and left it on the bar. The investigation after Peter died uncovered no sign of anyone else having been in the house between the time I made the drink at about 4:45 and when Peter came home at 5:00.

Rusty always accompanied me while I worked out in the pool house. We would enter the pool house and close the door to avoid straining the air conditioning. Rusty had plenty of water in the pool house and enjoyed being there with me. If he wanted to return to the house to greet Peter, he could use the dog door in the pool house and then the one in the kitchen. However, I always played loud rock music during my workouts, which meant the dog probably wouldn't have heard an intruder in the unlikely event one came to the house between 4:45 and 5:00. I always locked the kitchen door when I went to the pool house, since there had been a few robberies in the neighborhood over the years. The absence of any sign of forced entry led everyone involved in the case to rule out the unlikely presence of an intruder during the small window of time available to them.

I had reviewed this set of facts many times before, but this time, another piece of the puzzle came to mind just before I fell asleep. Peter and Rick often drank scotch together, and sometimes Rick would join Peter at our home for drinks before heading to his own place. The two men had been partners for eleven years, and Rick had come over for after-work scotch with Peter dozens of times. Rick was well aware of my habit of leaving a drink for Peter, and he showed up most often on my workout days. Drinks after work for the two partners were all about boys' time.

I went to bed, still struggling to piece things together. The next morning, when the buzzer went off to signal the start of the day for all the inmates at Estrella, I woke up with an epiphany—the dog door. What if someone had entered through it? The police forensic team had found a single strand of human hair stuck to the weather stripping on the dog door. They ran a DNA analysis, but found no matches. In 2004, the state of Arizona had only just begun requiring DNA testing of convicted felons, so the database was still far from extensive.

During my trial, Rachel had argued that the hair provided reasonable doubt that someone other than me could have entered the house and committed the murder, but there was no evidence of who that might be. The prosecution argued that this would have been highly unlikely, considering there was only a fif-teen-minute window (from 4:45 to 5:00 p.m.) for an intruder to enter through the dog door without being seen by myself or Peter. They claimed the hair could have come from many sources, tracing back to the dog door installation and including any guests we'd had over the years who might have brushed up against the weather stripping. Ultimately, the jury concluded that the sliver of doubt created by the human hair did not rise to reasonable doubt.

But none of that mattered to me anymore. Rick had attended my trial, so he was fully aware of the human hair evidence and that it had led nowhere. However, if I told the right story, I could use the hair to provoke Rick into making a statement closer to a confession. I was convinced he was involved in Peter's murder and desperate to prove it.

After breakfast, I asked a D.O. if I could make a private phone call. A pack of cigarettes helped ensure the answer was yes. I gave the number to the D.O., who then dialed it. When Rachel answered, the D.O. handed me the phone and stepped away for privacy. I explained my plan to Rachel and asked if she could help. Rachel said she would try. Now, all I had to do was wait for Rick to make his weekly visit and set my plan in motion. It was a do-or-die Hail Mary, but I had nothing to lose at that point. I'd been convicted and was going to spend the rest of my life in prison if I couldn't change the course of this rapidly flowing stream.

Rick showed up on a Thursday. By then, I'd been in custody for twenty-eight days, and my sentencing

Steven Decker

hearing was only two weeks away. Rick was dressed in his usual casual attire, a T-shirt and cargo shorts. He seemed calm and collected, but I intended to change that.

"Any news?" asked Rick.

"Oh yeah," I said. "It was a man, not a woman."

Rick's eyebrows went up. "How'd they find that out?"

"They found a match for the human hair that had been found on the dog door. They must have missed it before."

Rick's eyebrows went up but he tried to put on a cheerful face. "That's great news! Who was it?"

"I have no idea. All I know is they caught him. He confessed to everything."

Rick looked stunned, temporarily silenced by this disturbing news. But I had to give him credit. He didn't flinch. "Why'd he do it?" he asked.

And now for the noose over the head. "You know why, Rick."

"Why would I know?" he asked, his tone defensive.

"Because you paid him to do it. At least, that's what he says."

Rick pressed his lips together and shook his head. "I can't believe that asshole got caught."

"DNA from the hair on the dog door, dude. I guess it was a tight fit for him."

"What's the plan now?" he asked, getting fidgety in his seat.

"Police are on the way here. I guess you'll be taking my place soon."

"Not if I can help it." Rick slammed down the phone, bolted from his seat and disappeared from my sight.

I hung up the phone, feeling good about what I'd accomplished but also well aware that things were out of my hands from that point forward. I told the guard I was finished and was escorted back to my cell. All I could do then was wait for Rachel to contact me.

CHAPTER 8

RACHEL ARRIVED A few hours after Rick had rushed out of the jail. We met in one of the privileged visitation rooms, and Rachel updated me on what had happened since my encounter with Rick. "My P.I. followed him. He made a quick stop at his house and then went straight to the airport. He parked in short-term parking and entered Terminal 4, dragging a carry-on suitcase behind him. He went to the American Airlines ticket counter and bought a first-class, one-way ticket to Mexico City."

"Did they catch him?" I asked.

"A private investigator has no authority to make an arrest, Becky, and even if he were a police officer, there's currently no basis for arresting Rick."

"But he's obviously on the run! He confessed to the crime during our conversation on the recorded phone lines."

"Well, if you'll remember, I wasn't there, so what you're telling me is the first thing I've heard about a confession. Give me more details. What did he say? Please be precise."

"When I told him the hitman had been caught and asked him if it was worth it to him to have hired him, he looked miffed. He said, 'I can't believe that asshole got caught.' Those were his exact words."

"That's not a confession, Becky."

"Well, how about this? I told him the police were on their way to Estrella to arrest him. The last thing he said to me was, 'Not if I can help it.' Then he hung up the phone and hurried out of the visitation area."

"That's closer, especially when combined with his course of action after he left the jail. But it's not a slam dunk by any means."

My temper flared. "But it's obvious, Rachel! Rick had Peter killed!" I couldn't believe that Rick was going to get away, and worse, that Rachel thought we didn't have enough to set me free!

Rachel raised both hands in the air. "Hold on, Becky! Just hold on. We have a chance, a reasonable chance, to make this work. But let me explain how things will proceed from here. Okay?"

I settled down as best as I could. Rachel Cohen was a skilled attorney who had always been straight with me about my chances and how things worked. Now was the time to listen to what she had to say. I nodded, and Rachel laid it all out for me.

"I called the prosecutor on your case and told

him that we have potentially viable new evidence that might reveal the true murderer. He was skeptical, but I've known Ken a long time, and he knows I wouldn't lead him down a rabbit hole on something like this. What we need are the recordings. He can get them a lot faster than I can. I'm going to his office as soon as I leave here."

"But what about Rick? He's getting away!"

"Becky, we simply don't have enough time to prevent Rick from boarding that plane. After I get to Ken's office, it'll still take several hours to get the tapes, but in the meantime, I can go over my notes from our meetings so that he knows what to expect. Then we have to listen to the tapes to verify everything you're claiming. If it all checks out, which I'm sure it will, it'll be up to Ken whether this calls for further investigation so that law enforcement can pursue Rick. I'll also ask him to agree to a hearing before Judge Hernandez once we've listened to the tape."

"So you're talking about two different things, right?"

"Yes. One involves investigating a case against Rick, and the other involves convincing a judge that your case needs to be reopened."

"But if they just catch Rick, it'll all work out!"

"Please, Becky! We need to stay focused. Rick will get off that plane in Mexico City and either hop on another plane to an unknown destination or rent a car and drive away. We won't catch him. That's an FBI, Interpol, and God knows what other agencies problem now. But it's no longer a local police issue. Your case, however, is still within our jurisdiction. We want to get you out, and we have a chance to make that happen. I'm not making any promises, as setting aside a jury's verdict is a tough battle. But we do have a chance, and that's more than we had a few hours ago."

I slumped back in my chair. I was angry that Rick would escape, but in the end, what I wanted most was my freedom, and Rachel was telling me I had a chance at that. "So what now?" I asked.

"I've got to run to the prosecutor right now," said Rachel. "But listen to me, please. Now, more than ever, you need to be strong. First, you speak to no one about this. I mean that, Becky. Let me do my job. Second, none of this will go as quickly as you want. Be patient. Hang with me. I'll be back to update you regularly. Stay on your good behavior here. No trouble. That would spoil everything."

"Okay," I said. "I'll try."

Rachel's eyes flashed sharply. She pointed a single finger at me. "You'll do more than try, Becky. You will do as I say. Period. This is a chance that one in a million convicted criminals gets. Don't blow it. Let me handle this."

I took a deep breath. "I'll do everything you say. Thank you."

CHAPTER 9

August 13, 2004

SEVEN WEEKS PASSED. It was now the second week of August. I had been in jail for seventy-seven days. The court postponed my sentencing date while Rachel argued her motion about the new evidence over several weeks. Because the judges were busy with trials from Monday to Thursday each week, they only held such hearings on Fridays. Thus, despite needing only four days of testimony and arguments to decide my case, each hearing day meant an extra week in jail.

As the defendant, I could attend these hearings wearing jail clothes and shackles on my ankles. The judge had asked the sheriff's deputy if he would permit me to be uncuffed at the counsel table so I could take notes to give to my attorney as the hearings went on. The deputy agreed, allowing my hands and arms to be free of restraints.

I found the initial proceedings tedious, as they mostly revolved around arguments between Rachel and the prosecution about the validity of the motion. The prosecution argued that Rick Miller's statements and subsequent flight did not prove my innocence. They also emphasized the importance of the jury's verdict. Twelve individuals had listened patiently to the presentations from both sides and still found me guilty. Rachel focused on the new evidence, arguing that the jurors would have reached a different verdict if they had known about the recordings and Rick's later actions.

The legal jargon overwhelmed me, and I was exasperated that what I knew to be true—that Rick had orchestrated my husband's murder—seemed unimportant to everyone in the courtroom except me. When the hearing recessed for bathroom breaks and other administrative matters, I quietly expressed my concern to Rachel that the significance of my discovery was being overlooked. Rachel tried to be patient with me, but I could tell her sympathy for my frustration was wearing thin. Therefore, I forced myself to stay silent and endured the seemingly endless stream of legalese from both sides.

In the end, Judge Hernandez agreed to reopen the case, and even the prosecutor, Ken Logan, privately told Rachel that he was fine with the outcome. This action restored my pretrial presumption of innocence, removing my former status as a convicted murderer. Now, I was essentially facing a new trial based on the third-party defense that Rick had committed the crime. Although the trial would take months to begin, Judge Hernandez had agreed to release me on a one-million-dollar bond with ankle bracelet monitoring. I paid the required $100,000 and was free, for now.

The court set a new trial date for December 6, nearly four months away. I'd have time to put my life back together while I waited for my trial to begin, and I knew just where to start. The first thing I did was go to Rick and Katlin Miller's house to get my dog, Rusty, back. This contradicted Rachel's most significant warning: Do not speak with anyone about this case, especially not with the wife of the newly accused Rick Miller.

Katlin Miller answered the door when I rang the doorbell. Katlin wore stylish Pilates attire from Sleekfit Attire. She had tied her blonde hair up in a bun. Sporting sleek, firm arms and a tan, she'd clearly used the top cosmetic surgeons in the Valley. Katlin was four or five years younger than me, around twenty-five years old, and we had socialized regularly during the five years she'd been married to Rick.

I had no idea how Katlin would react upon seeing me, but I was happy to receive a cordial greeting from her. "Hi, Becky! I heard you'd gotten out. Good for you." Her voice sounded friendly but her expression seemed strained.

"Thanks, Katlin. Yes, I'm out for now."

"Well, since I haven't seen my husband in four weeks, I would assume you're on solid ground in your new trial. I mean, he told me he had an urgent business meeting in Omaha, Nebraska. Then the police came asking me if I knew he'd gone to Mexico. By the way, has anyone heard from him?"

"I certainly haven't," I said. "And I'm sorry about all of this. I'm here to pick up Rusty."

"Oh yes, absolutely. He's been great, by the way. Why don't you come in while I go get him? I actually wanted to speak with you, regardless."

Katlin turned away from the front door, leaving me to make a choice. I knew that coming here was against everything Rachel had warned me about. I was going to be on trial again for murder, and any encounter with a potential witness was ill-advised. Yet, I felt very alone now that I was out of jail, with no one to comfort me except my lovable dog. I wanted him back, and this seemed like the quickest way to make that happen.

I sensed something from the moment Katlin answered the door. She had something to tell me. Something important. Trusting my instincts, I entered the sprawling single-level home and followed Katlin to where she kept the dogs. Rusty was beside himself when he saw me, running to me and jumping up, standing on his back legs and propping his front legs against my chest. He licked my face with his soggy tongue as I held him in my arms. I'd been in jail for nearly three months, but my trusty Irish setter hadn't forgotten me.

"Why don't we have a seat here in the family room," Katlin suggested. "The kids are with my parents, so it's just me and the dogs." The Millers' golden doodle, Buster, sat in the corner, appearing frightened of the visitor. Known to be exceptionally timid, Buster had apparently gotten along well with Rusty during my absence. I sat on the sofa, and Katlin sat in an arm-chair across from me. "Can I get you something to drink?" she asked.

"Oh, no, thank you. You know, my attorney said I shouldn't talk to anyone involved in the case."

Katlin's expression now showed the tension I'd felt in her when standing at the front door. She seemed on the verge of tears but tried to hide it. "Yeah, I guess that's what they have to tell you. And I'm sure they're right. But I've felt so lost these past four weeks. I can't believe Rick would do this."

I suppose she didn't have many people to talk to about her problem, either, and I was glad she was open-ing up to me. "I'm sorry all of this happened," I said, and I meant it. "It would have been so much better if Peter were still alive and Rick hadn't..." I paused, not wanting to criticize Rick in front of Katlin. After all, I didn't know how she felt about him at this point, or me, and I tried to navigate out of the predicament my mouth had once again gotten me into. "What's going on, Katlin? How can I help you?"

"I think I know who Rick hired to do this," she said. "I didn't realize what was happening at the time, but now it makes sense."

Well, I didn't expect that! And I wasn't about to walk away from it. "Who do you think it was?"

Katlin explained. "You might not be aware of it since Rick is so successful, but he was raised in the Maryvale area of West Phoenix."

I sensed where this was going. Maryvale was a very rough section of town. And now that I thought of it, in all the years I'd known Rick, he'd never once mentioned his family. "So, you think the person he hired was from Maryvale?"

"He might be. Rick has a cousin, Mike Lester, who has a checkered past. He's been in and out of prison and he's a real black sheep in the family. No one from Rick's family ever talked to him, but one day, Mike's beat-up old pickup was parked in our driveway when I got home from the health club. When I came in, Rick looked surprised and told me Mike was just leaving. He shuffled Mike out really fast. I asked Rick what Mike was doing here, and he said he'd come over to beg for money. I asked him if he gave him any, and Rick said he had. To get rid of him. I asked him how much, and he didn't answer, like he was avoiding it, and he managed to get me off the subject. I never thought about it again until it became clear to me that Rick wasn't coming home."

"Did you tell the police about this?"

Katlin frowned. "No, I didn't. When they came to interview me, I still thought Rick was innocent. And I didn't even remember Mike being here when they came. But as time dragged on and I heard nothing from Rick, I realized it was probably true that he did this. And then I started thinking about things more deeply."

"But you'd tell the police now, right?"

"Yeah, sure."

"Do you know where this Mike Lester lives?" I asked.

"No, I don't, but I know where a few people from Rick's side of the family live. It shouldn't be too hard to track him down."

"And you think Rick might have hired this guy to kill Peter? Is that what you're saying, Katlin?"

"That's what I'm saying."

CHAPTER 10

December 16, 2004, 11 a.m.

RACHEL AND I had been sitting in the courthouse cafeteria since 9 a.m. while the jury deliberated. The judge had sent them to the jury room the day before, around 4 p.m. They spent an hour behind closed doors, and the judge adjourned them at 5 p.m. They reconvened at 9 a.m., adding another two hours to their deliberation. Just before eleven, Rachel's pager beeped. She recognized the number as belonging to the judge's secretary. Rachel looked me in the eye and said, "The jurors either have a question or they've reached a verdict. We need to get back to the courtroom."

We rushed back to the courtroom and took our seats at the defense counsel table. The prosecution and court staff had already taken their seats, and the judge was on the bench. "We have a verdict," said Judge Hernandez.

My heart raced. I'd been through a lot and now it would either all be over or I would go to prison for the rest of my life. They had indicted me for the murder of Peter Moreland in December 2003. I endured the first trial, a jury found me guilty, and I spent seventy-seven days in jail. The court released me in August 2004 because of new evidence regarding Rick Miller and the man he had hired to kill Peter, Mike Lester. The police easily tracked down Lester, and he confessed to the crime during his initial interrogation. He hoped that his willingness to implicate Rick as the mastermind behind Peter's murder would earn him favor with the prosecutor. The discovery that the DNA of the hair that had been found on the weatherstripping of my kitchen dog door matched Lester's DNA also motivated him to cooperate. The case looked promising for me, but Rachel urged me not to be overconfident, explaining that jurors could be difficult to predict.

"All rise," the judge announced. The gallery stood, as did the judge himself. The jury entered the courtroom. "Please be seated," said the judge. Everyone took their seats. "Has the jury reached a verdict?"

The jury foreperson stood. She was a woman in her thirties, dressed in slacks and a sweater. "We have, your honor."

"Please hand the verdict form to the bailiff."

The bailiff approached the jury box, where the foreperson handed him the document. He then walked the paper to the bench and presented it up to the judge. The judge read the verdict silently before passing the document to the clerk. "Will the defendant please rise for the reading of the verdict?" the judge asked.

Rachel and I stood. My heart was beating fast. *Here we go again,* I thought, drawing in a deep breath and holding it.

The clerk read the verdict. "On count one, murder in the first degree: not guilty."

I exhaled a tremendous sigh of relief, turned to Rachel, and hugged her. The one-year nightmare was over, except that Peter was still gone.

"Thank you for your service," said the judge, addressing the jury. Lost in thought, I barely heard him as he put the finishing touches on my trial. "You are excused, and the bailiff will escort you from the courtroom." The jury exited the courtroom, and the judge proceeded. "I'd like to thank both the prosecution and the defense for their handling of this retrial. You've conducted yourselves like true professionals. Ms. Moreland, I wish you all the best. The deputy will remove your ankle monitor; your bail is exonerated, and you are free to go. I hope that despite these difficult circumstances, you can build a life filled with meaning and happiness. This court is adjourned." The judge banged his gavel and stood to leave the courtroom. Everyone rose, the judge departed, and a buzz of animated conversations erupted.

As the gallery filed out, Rachel took me by the arm. "Stay close to me. The reporters are going to be all over you."

From the beginning, the press had portrayed me as the "socialite murderess." The media would never admit they'd been wrong, and I was reluctant to help them craft a new story about Rick Miller and Mike Lester.

"Do I have to speak with them?" I asked.

"You don't, but let's face it. Your reputation in the community has suffered. If you'd like to say something that you think might help restore it or be a building block for your life going forward, it's fine."

I liked that idea. "Okay, let's do it."

I made a few brief remarks to the print and radio reporters outside the courtroom. Then, when we were out on the courthouse steps, a horde of reporters, each followed by cameramen, confronted me. This is where I would use the press to my advantage. I knew exactly what I wanted to say. "Ladies and gentlemen, as of this morning, I am a free woman. It's been a long year, but unfortunately, this excellent result will not bring back my husband. I want to thank Rachel Cohen and her firm for defending my innocence. My faith in the justice system is strong, and at least one of the guilty parties will soon answer for what he's done."

"What will you do now?" a reporter yelled.

"Well, I'm not completely sure, but the thought

has crossed my mind that I might want to pursue investigative journalism. I have a degree in journalism from the Cronkite School at ASU, but I've never used it. Now that I've seen first-hand how things work, I'm intrigued. I think I can make a difference in the lives of other innocent people through investigative journalism."

The questions kept coming, and Rachel eventually leaned over and spoke into my ear. "Great job," she said. "This would be a really good time to stop, however." I finished up, and we pushed our way down the steps and into the parking garage across the street from the Courthouse. "Can I take you to lunch?" asked Rachel. "I know a great steakhouse nearby, Durant's."

"Sure," I said.

We made our way to the parking lot and got into our cars, and I followed Rachel to Durant's. A hostess seated us in a red-cushioned booth in the old-school steakhouse. I noticed people staring at us as we walked in and even while we were sitting, and I wondered how long it would take for the notoriety to wear off.

"You're pretty famous," said Rachel. "And I think your fame will be reframed positively now."

"How so?" I asked.

"Well, mainly because you essentially saved yourself. You took some chances, against my admonitions, I might add, and yet you were able to get to the truth. You're really a natural at this, Becky. Were you serious when you said you were thinking about pursuing investigative journalism?"

"I think so."

"Well, you did yourself a favor when you answered that reporter's question about what you want to do now that you're free. I wouldn't be surprised if you get a few calls about job offers."

"I'm not sure about that," I said. "I have no experience."

"True, but you're famous. That means something in the field of journalism."

"We'll see what happens," I said. "I'm just glad this ugly chapter in my life is over."

"It's over, but it's not over," Rachel said. "There will be emotional scars that may heal faster if you see a licensed therapist. Not everyone you encounter moving forward will support your innocence. Those kinds of interactions can be painful, and having a good therapist by your side can be beneficial."

"Thanks, Rachel. I really appreciate your advice. And I thank you from the bottom of my heart for sticking with me."

"I must admit that you've been a challenging client, Becky. Like most, you didn't understand how our legal system works. But because of your great instincts in reading people, you gathered evidence that allowed the system to provide you with the justice you deserve. It just took a little time."

"I get it," I said. "And it comforts me to know I live in a country where the legal system can work in most cases."

"And if you get into investigative journalism, you can help to enhance the system's effectiveness in those cases where it might have fallen short."

"Thanks for all your support and encouragement, Rachel."

"It's the least I can do. I want you to have a great life, and now you have the chance."

CHAPTER 11

WHEN I ARRIVED home, a platoon of reporters and camera crews confronted me. After forcing my way into my driveway, I quickly pulled the car into the garage and closed the garage door behind me. Thankfully, none of the reporters had been so bold as to follow my car into the garage, although a few had run up the driveway behind me, screaming questions. I wondered if that was what my career as an investigative reporter might look like. I certainly hoped not.

My message machine had dozens of messages. Most were congratulatory (from friends in the neighborhood and the country club), but three were from media companies that wanted to discuss job opportunities. One was from my mother.

My first instinct upon hearing my mother's voice was to skip through the message. After all, they refused to believe I hadn't been involved in Peter's murder. My parents were absurdly obsessed with social status. They attended the right church (the same one all their wealthy friends went to), made appearances at the appropriate charity events, and limited our social interactions to those with people from the same social class as ours. I was an only child, and while my parents indulged me, they instilled the rules of "proper behavior" in me from a young age.

When I met Peter shortly after graduating from college, my parents were thrilled. Peter came from a wealthy background, and though his business had just begun when we met, my parents believed he would be financially secure regardless of Sleekfit Attire's fate. Their approval of Peter only increased as his business grew. He could do no wrong in their eyes, and even when I informed them about his affair, they seemed to hold me responsible for not keeping him happy.

When Peter was murdered and the authorities accused me, everyone, including my parents, reached the same conclusions from the facts of the case. They severed all contact with me. I hadn't heard from them in over a year. But now that I was exonerated and had become somewhat of a celebrity, they probably dismissed all of that as a distant memory. At least, that's how it seemed based on the content of my mother's message:

"Rebecca, my dear, your father and I were simply elated when news came to us of your innocence. What a nightmare this past year must have been for you.

Please call us to let us know you're all right and to make plans to get together as soon as humanly possible. We've missed you terribly and want so very much to see you. Sending all our love. We hope to hear from you soon. Bye."

You can imagine how I felt at that moment. Knowing my parents had forsaken me, despite my innocence, was profoundly hurtful. I had no intention of replying to their message with any urgency. Instead, I considered the messages about job opportunities in greater detail.

As I mentioned, three companies had left messages for me: the leading local newspaper in Phoenix, a national tabloid, and a reputable international news agency. Although I wasn't interested in working for a tabloid, I found the local newspaper appealing because I wanted to stay in Phoenix and believed it could be a better place to start my career than a large, high-pressure international company. But it wouldn't hurt to hear what the larger company had to say. I returned the calls from both the local and international companies and scheduled interviews.

During both interviews, I conveyed my desire to pursue stories that would allow me to uncover evidence that might help wrongfully accused individuals win their cases. To my surprise, both interviewers said my focus on those kinds of cases wouldn't generate much news. When I asked why, they explained that the overwhelming majority of accused people are actually guilty. This was disappointing but not a deal killer for me. I wanted a job. Thus, it became essential to leverage what I had to offer (my fame, no matter how fleeting) to negotiate a job description that would enable me to follow my passion while also providing value, i.e., news for my employer. In the end, believe it or not, the large international company proved to be more flexible. This might have been because they weren't struggling to survive, as were so many local newspapers at the time.

My employer agreed that I could pursue my personal agenda while also being responsible for regularly submitting viable news stories. The intentional vagueness of "regularly" in my contract benefited me. Although I preferred reporting on wrongly accused innocents, my editor clarified that my time would inevitably be consumed by cases involving undeniably guilty people. I wasn't convinced of that but certainly didn't want to be chasing people up their driveway trying to get a quote for a story. Thus, I secured a concession excusing me from taking part in scenes like the one in front of my home that I experienced just after my release. Instead, my role would be more subtle, taking advantage of my status as an innocent victim wrongly accused. The trust that subjects would have in me was expected to be more substantial than that in a typical reporter; at least, that was the hope. I vowed to never forget how poorly the press had treated me during my first trial and subsequent conviction, and to avoid treating others that way, regardless of the circumstances.

My start date was February 1, 2005. I would spend my first month in NYC, attending a training class on Investigative Reporting. This gave me over a month to spend time with Rusty and to find someone to watch him while I was away. The need for a dog sitter for Rusty sparked an idea: I would ask my parents to take care of him. After all, they had a lot to make up for if I was ever going to allow them to reenter my life.

CHAPTER 12

THE NEXT MORNING, I woke at 5:30 a.m., as was my habit during the winter months in Phoenix. When the summer heat encroached, I'd reset the alarm to 4:30 a.m. I had a quick cup of coffee, and at 5:55, I left the house through the gate in the back wall of the courtyard. I always locked the gate, but I had no doubt that Mike Lester had climbed over it or scaled the wall to enter my home on the day he murdered Peter. But Mr. Lester was locked away for life now, and I didn't have to worry about him bothering me at home, ever again.

People who are unfamiliar with Phoenix often have no idea that the area boasts 180 miles of canals, surpassing the combined canal systems of Venice and Amsterdam. The ancient Hohokam people, who disappeared around 1450, built the original canal system here in the Valley of the Sun, to irrigate crops. Their successors, the Pima and Hopi tribes, continued this practice. Modernization and renovation have transformed the canals into excellent locations for biking, walking, and running. They are much cleaner than before, thanks to the introduction of the White Amur, a special kind of carp from China that consumes nearly its entire body weight in algae and weeds each day.

Rusty pranced alongside me as we turned left onto the canal. As always, runners, cyclists, and other walkers were out, trying to get some exercise before heading to work. Ducks swam in the canal, hunting for fish. I spotted one up ahead that had climbed onto the hard-packed sandy road beside the water, quacking and eating breadcrumbs dropped by a friendly lady. Rusty showed no interest in the duck, opting instead to sniff at the scents left by other animals from the night before.

As I walked along, gazing at the Praying Monk in the distance (a hundred-foot-tall rock formation on Camelback Mountain that resembled a monk kneeling in prayer), my thoughts turned inward. Until my ordeal over the past year concluded, I hadn't been able to appreciate my freedom, but now I treasured it. I breathed in the fresh morning air and exhaled with enthusiasm.

This was the first day of the rest of my life, and I wanted to enjoy it. But that no longer meant being content with walking the dog and working out in the pool house gym. I needed to take life seriously, to become a productive citizen—and for once, I truly believed I would. Nothing would stop me from pursuing my new goals. Looking back, I can't help but marvel at my naivety. I wasn't chasing a fresh start. I was running straight into a reckoning. And it was coming for me far sooner than I could have imagined.

CHAPTER 13

INVITED MY PARENTS over for cocktails, and they
arrived promptly at 4 p.m. I took them into the
den and served them their drinks. My mother
preferred white wine, so I bought an expensive bottle
of California chardonnay for the occasion. My father
enjoyed scotch, and I got him a bottle of twelve-year-
old Macallan. It wasn't the same brand of scotch that
had been the vehicle for Peter's murder, but I couldn't
help but think of him when I bought that bottle for
my father. But I shrugged it off. After all, the police
had locked away the bottle that had killed Peter in
an evidence closet, very likely never to be seen again.

Once my parents had their drinks and were seated
on the sofa, I sat in the armchair across from them,
holding a glass of my favorite Sauvignon Blanc. Now
was the moment for my shock and awe campaign to
begin. "I suppose you both know this is the room
where Peter was poisoned," I said.

Both of them responded with raised eyebrows. My
mother, Lydia Greystone, a fifty-nine-year-old woman

with beautifully dyed blonde hair, fit and trim from her time at the gym, now looked distinctly uncomfortable. When she had entered the house, she was full of joy and good tidings, with Christmas just around the corner and her daughter's freedom to celebrate. All of that vanished when my terse words reached their ears.

My father, Barnabas Greystone III, in his mid-sixties, was a large, balding man. Though he always dressed impeccably, he could no longer hide the pot belly he had cultivated over a lifetime of fine dining and excessive drinking. He played golf three times a week, and while he still walked the course during the fall and winter, when the temperatures allowed, the exercise couldn't offset the effects of endless indulgence.

As for me, I felt no queasiness while in the den or in the house overall. Though I had loved Peter and missed him, my time in jail significantly toughened me. I was no longer the delicate wallflower I had been before the ordeal. Frankly, it felt wonderful to be home again and free. But I digress. I was telling you about my first meeting with my parents since they had abandoned me over a year earlier. I let them sweat for a while, remaining silent and planning to stay that way until one of them spoke. As always, my mother didn't disappoint.

"Maybe we should sit by the pool, Rebecca. We shouldn't waste this beautiful weather. Remember, summer is just around the corner!" She chuckled softly, attempting to lighten the mood.

I had no intention of cooperating. "I prefer it inside, mother. I've gotten used to being inside over the past year. With my time in jail and all."

My mother grimaced. My father made his case more bluntly. "I think your mother might feel uncomfortable in this room, Rebecca, for obvious reasons."

I refused to accept that. In the past, I had always given in to my father's demands, but not anymore. "What on earth could make you uncomfortable, Mother? You always loved this room."

She scrunched up her lips, now perturbed. "Never mind," she said, leaning forward and glaring at me, undoubtedly perturbed by my newfound stubbornness. While living a pampered life, Lydia Greystone could be one tough lady when circumstances demanded it. After all, she had abandoned her only daughter in her time of need. I would think a person would need very thick skin to do that.

My father was the same. I knew he was uncomfortable, yet his expression remained stoic. He would persevere, giving me hope I could reach them. And so I began. "I need to say something to both of you, and you need to hear me. Please don't interrupt."

Nods. They must have been prepared to face the consequences of their actions, and now I would deliver them. "It's crucial for us to be in this room together because this is where our ordeal began. This is the place where something happened that led to my imprisonment and caused you two to abandon me." My mother winced slightly. My father didn't move a muscle. "And while I have yet to hear an apology from either of you or any sign of remorse for your horrific treatment of your only child, I have to believe you wouldn't be here unless you wanted to." Nearly imperceptible nods from both of them. "But before you do that, I want to share something that happened to me in jail more than once.

My father raised his hand and pressed his palm toward me. "That's not necessary, Rebecca. We understand your ordeal must have been a living hell."

I widened my eyes and glared at him. "You need to hear this." My father lowered his hand and leaned back on the sofa, allowing me to continue. "During my seventy-seven days at Estrella, I had a variety of cellmates. They came and went. But when they left, none were going home. When they rolled up their grimy little mattresses and disappeared, they were headed to Perryville, the prison where they would serve their sentence. Some of them will remain there for the rest of their lives." I paused. My parents seemed frozen, their lips pressed together, both eager yet reluctant to hear more. "That's what would have happened to me if I hadn't stumbled upon a way to save myself."

"And you did it brilliantly," said my father. A compliment. Rare indeed. I suppose I was making progress.

I could have replied, "*No thanks to you,*" but I let it

slide. "Let me finish my story, please, and then we can talk." A nod from my father. "The sad fact is that nearly all of my cellmates were guilty, yet almost every one of them received regular visits from their parents. I remember one cellmate who had visits every day from her mother, and after each visit, she'd return to our cell in tears. Tears of guilt for what she'd done to her mom, but also tears of hope. Her mom had promised her she was raising money for her appeal, assuring her that she would hire the best lawyer in town to help. You may wonder how that made me feel." I raised my eyebrows. My parents were frowning, bracing for the blow. "I mean, the woman was guilty, without a doubt. She'd murdered her cheating husband in cold blood in front of witnesses. There was no chance an appeal would even be granted for her; she was going to prison for the rest of her life." A pause. "But her mom still came to see her every day."

I give my father credit. Chalk it up to a lifetime of therapy sessions, but he took a deep breath and said the right words. "How did that make you feel?"

"It made me feel very alone in this world, Dad. My husband was dead; no one from this make-believe world here in Paradise Valley wanted to have anything to do with me, including my parents. So it was just me and my attorney against the world. I was buying off predatory inmates on the inside with candy bars and cigarettes while you two were dining out with your fake friends at the country club. And now, I have a question, and I want you both to answer it. How does that make *you* feel?"

My heart was racing because, like any child, I wanted to believe my parents loved me. However, in my case, they had done something that made that seem impossible. I was offering them a chance to make things right, but I had no idea what words they could use to accomplish that—probably none. Still, I wanted to give them the opportunity to try.

"I'll go first," said my father, sitting up straight. "You ask how does it make me feel, Becky. And if I am honest, I can say I feel many things. First, I feel pride for what you accomplished in the most difficult circumstances. I also feel sadness for what you experienced. But most of all, I feel shame for failing you when you needed me most. I apologize from the bottom of my heart, and I will spend the rest of my life trying to prove how much I love you."

My father did not shed a tear, but his words hit home. I believed him, but I needed to clarify something. "Money won't prove it, Dad. You know that, right?" He nodded. My eyes turned to my mother, who had a pained expression on her face. "Mom?"

My mother's voice trembled as she tried to cull together some words that might have meaning to me. "I agree with your father. I was a fool." She lowered her head, shaking it from side to side. Her hand went to her face, and she cried quietly but wasn't done. She raised her head and looked at me, tears spilling from her gray-blue eyes. "I'm so sorry, Becky. I'm so ashamed."

I gave my mother some time to compose herself. Rusty, whom I had put outside because of my mother's allergies, was scratching at the door. I had locked the infamous dog door permanently and would soon have the entire door replaced. I went to let him in. After all, my mother's "allergies" really stemmed from a dislike of dogs (and cats). We had never had a pet when I was growing up. Perhaps now was the time to put that ruse to an end.

Rusty rushed into the den and went to my parents. My father cuddled his head in his hands for a moment, and my mother even reached over and pet him lightly. To me, this was a sign that things were going to be different between my parents and me from then on.

"Are you okay, Mom? Can I get you some more wine?"

My mother sat up, dabbing her tears with a tissue from the coffee table.

"I'm fine, thank you. And yes, wine would be wonderful. It's delicious, by the way. Now, tell me, dear, what are your plans?"

Perfect segue, Mom. Thanks! I got up to pour the wine while speaking. "I've taken a job as an investigative reporter. It starts on February 1."

My parents sat back, surprised. I could tell they struggled to decide how to respond. Should they congratulate me or admonish me? My father took the lead. "How did this come about?" he asked, a tepid smile on his face.

"Well, Dad, I'm famous now. In a good way, you know. I'm an innocent victim who essentially saved herself. And when the media interviewed me after the verdict, I mentioned that I was interested in investigative journalism. You two remember I have my degree in that, right?"

"Yes, yes, of course," said my father. "Are they going to allow you to stay in Phoenix? I certainly hope so."

"They are. I have to go to New York for a month of training. But after that, I'll be stationed in Phoenix, reporting on crime, racial injustice, political corruption, and corporate wrongdoing in the region. Which is one reason I asked you over. I need your help while I'm away."

"How so?" asked my father.

"I need you to watch Rusty while I'm gone."

My father didn't hesitate. "That should be fine."

My mother was less enthusiastic. "But you realize our home isn't set up for pets, dear? We have no fence. Poor Rusty wouldn't be safe."

I sat back in my chair. "I want you to live here, Mom, while you care for Rusty. It'll only be a month."

My home was lovely, but it paled in comparison to

the majestic palace where my parents lived, high on Camelback Mountain. The view of Phoenix and the surrounding mountains was spectacular, and having live-in servants was a feature of daily life they had grown dependent on.

Again, my father came to the rescue. "We'll be happy to come here for a month, Becky."

"And you won't just have your servants do it, right?" I asked. "I'd really like you two to get to know Rusty. He's a great dog."

My mother had a forced smile, but my dad seemed genuinely excited about staying here for a month. "That sounds good to me," he said.

"And you, Mom? Are you able to be here to keep Dad and Rusty company?"

After a pause, my mother jumped in. "Absolutely, dear. It's the least we can do after the terrible mistakes we made."

CHAPTER 14

I SPENT JANUARY 2005 addressing issues concerning Peter and Rick's company, Sleekfit Attire. The business had been in limbo since Rick had disappeared and became the chief suspect in Peter's murder. The life insurance company had withheld payouts until my innocence or guilt was determined. Even worse, the absence of a general manager caused mid-level managers to struggle to keep the company running until my case concluded.

In January, I sought a court order to hire a management firm to oversee the company's daily operations and search for a buyer. One of the first recommendations from the consultants was to change all access codes for the company's bank accounts and computer systems, preventing Rick from withdrawing funds overseas or interfering with the company in any other way.

My acquittal in December 2004 finally allowed the disbursement of Peter's insurance money to me. I was the policy's original beneficiary, but the initial guilty verdict disqualified me. The insurance issue was now settled, but complications arose regarding the ownership of the company. The company lawyers informed me I was the rightful recipient of both Peter's and Rick's stock based on their interpretation of the company's operating agreement. Rick's breach of fiduciary duty to the company meant his stock rightfully belonged to me. If this happened, I would become the sole owner of Sleekfit Attire.

I was concerned that Rick's wife, Katlin, would be left out in the cold. In this situation, no provision in the company by-laws would allow Rick's stock to transfer to her. However, the attorneys informed me that nothing stopped me from compensating Katlin with a onetime goodwill payment from the company or from the funds I received from the sale of the company or from other sources.

Kaitlin had been facing financial difficulties since Rick's disappearance, and I had been assisting her by providing loans from my personal accounts. Clearly, this wasn't a sustainable solution, so I decided to move forward quickly with the paperwork that would grant me 100% ownership of Sleekfit Attire. My next directive was for the management firm to expedite the sale, which they could now easily accomplish, since the company's ownership had been finalized. A prospective buyer sent a letter of intent by the end of January; we expected to complete the sale in March or April, after their final due diligence.

With the company's issues behind me, I visited Katlin Miller's home. I informed her that the sale of the company was pending and that I would provide her with a substantial cash infusion once it closed. I felt she deserved this, since Rick's heartless actions had left her with nothing. Knowing she would remain short on funds until the company sale closed, I wrote her a check to tide her over for the next few months and told her I'd ask my attorney to apply it to her loan balance. I also informed her I would go to New York for a month and that my parents would stay at my house to look after Rusty. She said she'd be happy to take him, but I told her I wanted my parents to show me a little love and step up to help. Katlin understood, as she was well aware of my parents' lack of sympathy for my situation until I identified Rick as the perpetrator of the crime.

As the end of January approached, I concentrated on packing for my month-long trip to New York, as I had only a few days to get ready. While rummaging through my medicine cabinet for ibuprofen, I noticed a small white bottle with a blue cap on one shelf. I didn't recognize it and had no recollection of placing it there. The bottle had no labels or identifying marks. I picked it up, shook it, and heard the pills rattling inside. I twisted off the cap and saw it was full. I poured a few of the pills into my hand and examined them to see if I could identify them. It was easy.

The pills displayed the molded letters "XANAX" on their white, rectangular, scored surfaces. These were the same kind I used to take, but I hadn't refilled the prescription after Peter's death. I had never used it much, anyway. But here was a full bottle sitting in my medicine cabinet. I couldn't understand how the pills got there. Had someone entered my home without my knowledge? Or had they been there for a long time, and I simply didn't remember them? Unfortunately, I had no time to investigate further. I placed the bottle back on the shelf and went on packing.

A month later, I would wish I had thrown them away.

PART 2

CHAPTER 15

February 2005

M Y TRAINING EXPERIENCE in New York was exceptional. Not only did I learn a great deal about investigative journalism, but I also formed new friendships. I must admit that my notoriety as a wrongfully convicted person and my journey to freedom influenced my initial experiences in the professional world. All the trainees and our instructors were familiar with my story, and while I didn't appreciate being treated differently, I believe it helped foster their patience with my lack of experience.

Everyone I met had a background in journalism. Some trainees had experience at newspapers that had shut down and seemed more like they could teach the classes rather than take them. The instructors were from the editorial and production teams, and many had worked as investigative reporters earlier in their careers.

I was to report to an editor named Tilly Blankenship. She was around forty years old and lived in New York with her husband, whom she said worked in finance. I got the impression that they were doing well financially. While I didn't know how much news agency editors earned, I assumed it wasn't enough to support a lavish lifestyle. Tilly and Rob lived in a three-bedroom apartment that probably cost over $10,000 a month to rent, so either one or both must have been making a lot of money or came from wealth. They frequently ate out, which is also ridiculously expensive in New York, and invited me to join them several times.

Tilly was a kind soul, and we really bonded during my month in the City. While I learned a lot in the classes, I gained even more from my time spent with Tilly. Because of my lack of journalistic experience, she said I'd have to work hard to improve my writing to the level of my colleagues. She suggested I do additional work outside of class, offering to help me with it. She encouraged me to read stories written by our company's journalists and then suggested I write a few stories myself. Her edits on my work, though initially daunting with all the red ink, ultimately sped up my writing development.

One day, toward the end of my training, I asked Tilly a question while we were out to lunch. "Hey, if you could share one piece of advice that could really make a difference for me in this profession, what would it be?"

Tilly sat back in her chair, thinking. She was a slim and fit brunette, impeccably dressed in a cashmere sweater, a black mid-length skirt, and leather boots. After a few seconds, she smiled and spoke. She had a smooth, southern accent, having been born and raised in New Orleans. "Who would know?" she said.

I was confused. "Know what?"

"Who would know the answer you're seeking? Let's say that a professor is accused of sexually abusing a student during private meetings in his office. Of course, the student making the accusation knows, but we can't be sure she's telling the truth. Who else might know?"

I thought about it. "Other students?"

"Certainly, but which ones? There could be hundreds of them. And how can you gain access to them?"

"I don't know."

"Here are two possibilities you can easily access: the professor's secretary and the janitor. If the professor has a history of this behavior, those two would likely have seen or heard something. For all we know, the secretary herself might be a victim of his advances."

Hmmm. I didn't think of that. I'd take those three words to heart and file them away. *Who would know?*

I was having dinner with Tilly the day before my training ended, just the two of us. We liked this little bistro called *La Bouchée Savoureuse*. The food was simple,

relatively inexpensive, and delicious. We also appreciated the wine selection. One thing I learned right
away about the journalism industry is that drinking
is a way of life for many. According to Tilly, the job's
stress drives this behavior—not just the pressure of
deadlines, editorial rules, and job security, but also
the nature of the stories themselves. Approaching
people with tough questions, particularly those who
have something to hide, is difficult. There's the risk of
retribution from those who feel harmed or misrep-
resented by the published work of journalists. These
factors contribute to a drinking culture that is hard to
ignore and difficult to resist.

Tilly and I were finishing our lunch that day when
my phone rang. It was my mother. "Becky, your father
is dead," she said. Her voice was exceptionally calm.

"How?" I asked, in shock.

"He died out on the canal while walking Rusty.
Rusty came back to the gate, and I heard him barking
furiously. I went out there and found your father. He
was...gone."

I was heartbroken and stunned. Still, Tilly was there
and undoubtedly wondering what was going on. "Hold
on a sec, Mom." I covered the phone and explained to
Tilly what had happened. Her face dropped, but she
remained silent. I put the phone back to my ear. "I'm
back. When... did it happen?"

"A few hours ago."

"What was it? Do they know?"

"They think it was a heart attack, but they're saying they might need to do an autopsy. They're asking questions, like if I know of anyone who might hold a grudge against Barney."

"Who's asking that?" I asked.

"The police, of course."

"How did they get involved?"

"I called 911, and the police showed up around the same time as the EMTs. The police asked if I was there when he died, and I said no. Then they said it was an unattended death, so they're referring it to the County Medical Examiner. They said they'll probably do an autopsy. I'm confused, Becky! What should I do?"

"Can you give me a second, Mom?" I put the phone down again. I was struggling to think. The shock of hearing that my father had died while doing something I had asked him to do was hitting me hard. The guilt was overwhelming.

Tilly stepped in to help, direct and to the point. "What does she need from you right now?"

"I think she wants to know if there's any reason for them to do an autopsy."

"Absolutely," said Tilly.

"Why?" I asked.

"You never know what it might yield," she said. "It's an unattended death, so they'll probably do it anyway, especially considering what happened at your home to

Peter. The home is obviously well known to the police due to all the notoriety of your case."

I put the phone up to my ear again. "Yes, Mom, tell them you have no objections to autopsy. Are you okay?"

"I'm fine, dear. I'm in a bit of shock, but okay. Rusty has been a great comfort to me."

"Okay, listen. I'm going to fly home today. I'll let you know about my flight times. I'll be there as soon as I can."

"Thank you, Becky."

"Hang in there, Mom. I love you.

"I love you too."

I ended the call and looked at Tilly, shaking my head. She reached over and touched my hand. "I'm so sorry, Becky."

"Thank you," I said. "Why were you so sure that an autopsy should be done?"

"I don't know," she said. "Maybe it's just our profession. Autopsies are an essential source of information. We always push for an autopsy when consulted. Even when we aren't consulted."

"Do you think foul play might be involved?" I asked.

"Well, think about what happened to your husband," said Tilly. "Could it happen again, but this time to your father?"

I considered this improbable hypothesis. My father

was a scotch drinker. Rick had hired Mike Lester to poison Peter by tampering with his scotch. Rick had escaped and had been missing for a year, and Mike Lester was serving a life sentence. Of the two, only Rick could have been involved in the murder of my father. But I kept the dog door locked now. He couldn't have gotten in that way. Oh no. The dog door! I picked up my phone again and called my mother. When she answered, I asked her a question. "Mom, you kept the dog door closed, right?"

"Why no, actually, we didn't. We found it quite convenient to have Rusty letting himself in and out of the house. Why do you ask?"

I didn't want to alarm my mother, but I also wanted to protect her. "No reason, but I'd prefer if you closed it and kept it locked. Rusty needs to learn to stay put for longer periods. Can you do that for me, Mom?"

"Yes, certainly. If you insist."

"Okay, thanks. I'll see you soon. Are you okay? Can you call a friend to sit with you for a while?"

"Yes, Andrea Peterson is on the way over now. I hope you don't mind."

"No, it's a good idea. Be safe. I'll be there soon."

I ended the call, anxious to leave New York. Tilly asked me if I was all right, placing her hand over mine as we sat there in the restaurant.

The touch of Tilly's hand on mine was comforting. "I want to cry, but I also want to find out how this happened. It'll probably hit me harder when I get home. Can you let the team know why I have to leave with only one day left in training?"

"Yes, of course," she said. "Uh, can I ask you something?"

"Certainly, Tilly, anything."

"Will you keep me up to date on the autopsy results? Especially the blood analysis?"

"Are you thinking what I think you are?" I asked. At that moment, I remembered the unmarked bottle of Xanax pills I had found in my medicine cabinet just before I left for New York. *Oh crap!*

"I'm not ruling anything out, are you?" she asked.

"Definitely not."

CHAPTER 16

COULDN'T CATCH A flight that day but was on the first one out the next morning. I arrived at Phoenix Sky Harbor Airport just before noon and took a taxi to my home in Paradise Valley. It was depressing to see crime scene tape wrapping around my yard and blocking my driveway. Two police cars were parked along the curb in front of my house, their lights flashing. A local news crew lurked nearby, where a cameraman filmed a newswoman reporting.

I asked the taxi driver to move a few houses down from my home. Retrieving my suitcase from the trunk, I opened it and put on my winter coat, which I'd been using back east. I zipped up the suitcase and paid the driver, pulled the hood of my jacket over my head, and approached my home, trying to keep as far away from the reporter and cameraman as I could.

As soon as I ducked under the crime scene tape, a uniformed police officer confronted me. "This a crime scene, ma'am. I can't let you enter."

"I'm the homeowner," I explained.

The officer hesitated, thinking. "Move behind the tape. I'll be back."

As soon as I was outside the taped area, the reporter and cameraman swooped in. I recognized the reporter, who'd interviewed me more than once. She held up her microphone as she rushed toward me. "Rebecca Moreland! Can we ask you a few questions?"

"No comment," I said, turning away, but the reporter didn't relent.

"Can you tell us what's going on here, Rebecca? This is your home, isn't it? We've heard there was a suspicious death here yesterday." The reporter extended her microphone toward me, as if she really expected me to answer her questions.

"No comment," I said. Thankfully, the police officer was now walking briskly down my driveway, waving for me to come back under the tape. I dipped under and approached him, leaving the reporter unsatisfied and wheeling my suitcase behind me.

"Come with me," he said, turning toward the house.

I followed the police officer into the house. I left my bag in the house's foyer, and the officer led me into the kitchen. A plainclothes detective approached me. "I'm Detective Sanders," he said. "Do you mind answering some questions, Ms. Moreland?"

"Where's my mother?" I asked.

"She's been returned to her home, along with the dog."

"I'm not willing to answer any questions without my lawyer being present."

The detective pressed his lips together. "All right. But you'll need to remain here until she arrives."

"Are you arresting me?" I asked.

"You're a person of interest," he said. "We'd like to speak with you."

"Okay then, I'm leaving. I need to go see my mother."

A person of interest is someone the police are investigating or would like to speak with regarding a crime, but who hasn't been arrested or charged. This individual may possess information about the crime or have a close relationship with the victim. A suspect is someone the police believe has committed a crime, with evidence pointing toward them as the perpetrator. Often, police arrest and charge a suspect when they believe they possess sufficient evidence. I'd been through this rigmarole before and had learned a few lessons. First, I didn't have to answer questions, whether I was a person of interest or a suspect. Second, if I answered questions to clear myself of any wrongdoing, I was entitled to have my attorney present. Most importantly, I wasn't being arrested or charged with a crime, so I was free to leave if I wanted to.

"Would it be helpful to you if I explained what's going on, ma'am?" asked the detective, trying to keep from leaving.

"Yes, it would." Obviously.

"We got an expedited tox screen on your father. It showed a lethal amount of a prescription drug in his system."

Oh boy. My thoughts flashed to the Xanax bottle from my medicine cabinet. I didn't want to disclose that, but maybe they already had it. Perhaps I could find out.

"What else?" I asked.

"We interviewed your mother this morning before taking her home."

"What did she say?"

"She said he had a few drinks after lunch, then took the dog for a walk. He never came home, but the dog did. She went looking for him and found his body lying on the canal path."

"Did my mother say what Dad had been drinking?"

The detective nodded. "Scotch."

This was turning into a nightmare, but I had to find out more. "Where is the scotch bottle now?"

"It's been seized as evidence."

"Has anything else been taken from my home?"

"Yes."

"All right, thank you, Detective Sanders. I'll be at my mother's." They probably had the Xanax bottle from my medicine cabinet, but I dare not ask about that. I'd have to speak with Rachel to figure out a strategy that would hopefully keep me from being arrested.

The detective interrupted my thought process. "How are you getting there? I'd be happy to drive you."

"I'll just take my car. It's in the garage."

"I'm sorry, Ms. Moreland, but we're still processing the scene, including the car."

"All right, I'll call a cab."

"It's really no trouble," he said.

I looked him straight in the eye. "No thank you."

"Okay," he said. "Here's my card. Please call me if you have any information you'd like to share with us."

Detective Sanders handed me a card, and I left the house. I stayed inside the tape to avoid further pestering from the reporter and called a cab. While I waited for the taxi, I reached out to Rachel on her personal cell. Rachel told me she could meet me at my mother's house in an hour. The cab arrived, and I departed, wondering if history was repeating itself. Or worse.

CHAPTER 17

MY MOTHER WAS doing okay. She met me at the door and hugged me tightly. I couldn't remember the last time she'd embraced me like that. Had she ever? Rusty was beside her. He greeted me with tail wagging and feet tapping, and then followed us to the back of the house. We sat in the room my parents called the "Quiet Room." Through the floor-to-ceiling windows, all you could see was the stark brown rock face of Camelback Mountain. My mother sat on the sofa, and Rusty jumped up beside her and nuzzled his head on her leg. Hmmm. I didn't allow him on the furniture in my home. Oh well, a subject for another time.

"I don't know what I would have done without Rusty," said my mother.

"I'm glad he was there for you, Mom."

"Can he stay for a while?" Here, with me?"

"Sure. Do you think I could stay, too? I won't be able to sleep in my house while it's a crime scene."

"Of course you can, dear. How long will the police be in your home?"

"I don't know, Mom. Last time, it was several days. Maybe Rachel will know more."

"Who's Rachel?"

"She's my attorney. Rachel Cohen. I hope you don't mind, but she'll be here in around thirty minutes. I'm a person of interest in the case and need representation."

"So am I," she said. "I suppose I'll need representation as well. Can Rachel represent both of us?"

"I don't think so, Mom. I'm happy to ask, but she'll probably refer you to another attorney she thinks would do a good job."

"All right. Your father and I use Snell and Wilmer. They've got hundreds of attorneys and a bunch of them are litigators."

"I don't think they're the right firm for this, Mom. I'm pretty sure they don't do criminal law at all."

"How do you know?" she asked.

"Rachel and I talked a lot about the law while I was on trial. I remember a few tidbits about which firm does what here in town. Anyway, before Rachel arrives, can you tell me what happened when the police arrived? When did they come?"

"Around ten this morning. There were two police cars and a few unmarked cars. The police in uniforms got out and started putting the crime scene tape around the yard while the detectives came to the door.

I answered, and they handed me a warrant to search the premises. They told me I was a person of interest and asked if they could ask me some questions."

"Did you agree to that?"

"Yes. Why shouldn't I? I have nothing to hide."

"It's okay, Mom, but from now on, don't answer questions unless your attorney advises you to, and only speak to them with your attorney present."

My mother nodded.

"Anyway, what did they want to know?"

"They wanted to know what Barney had been doing before the walk, what time he left the house, what time I found him, things like that."

"Anything else?"

"They asked if he'd seemed tired, or ill, before the walk."

"Did he?"

"Not that I remember. He seemed okay. He always gets a little sluggish after he drinks, and he'd had a few. You know he's always been a big drinker."

"Yeah. It was scotch, right?"

"Yes."

"Do you know if it was the bottle I bought for you when you came to see me in December? I know it was still there when I left for my trip."

"Oh no, Barney finished that one in just a few days. Then he went home and brought some of his supply. He drinks Dewar's thirty-seven-year-old." She grimaced and lowered her head, realizing she'd said "drinks" rather than "drank."

I reached out and placed my hand on top of hers, trying to comfort her. "Did they take the bottle from the house? The one he'd been pouring from that day?"

"Yes, they did."

"Did you see them take anything else?"

"Yes, I saw them come down from the bedroom area with a clear plastic bag. There was a white pill bottle in it. I don't know what kind of pills."

But I did. Why hadn't I just washed them down the sink? Who knew where this would lead? Just then, the doorbell rang. It was Rachel. I introduced her to my mother, and she quickly clarified that she couldn't represent her. She pulled out a pad from her briefcase and wrote down three attorney's names for my mom, urging her to call them immediately. My mom agreed and told us she'd go to another part of the home while we met in the Quiet Room. To my surprise, Rusty went with my mom instead of staying with me. Rachel and I sat down and got down to business.

"Tell me what you know," said Rachel.

I told her what I'd learned from my mother and the detective. She knew that I'd been in New York for the past month from our phone call. But she didn't know about the Xanax, and while I dreaded doing so, I went ahead and told her. "Rachel, there's something really strange that happened a few days before I left for New York."

Rachel's eyebrows raised. "What's that?"

"I found an unmarked pill bottle in my medicine cabinet. I opened the bottle, and it was full of Xanax pills."

"Do you know where the pills came from?"

"No idea. I should have thrown them away, right?"

"I don't think so. You should have reported it, Becky."

"To who?"

"The police. If you didn't put the pill bottle there, then who did? How did they gain entry to your home? Considering what you just went through over the past year, what were you thinking? You didn't handle the bottle, did you?" I sheepishly nodded my head. "Oh, great! Odds are the bottle was clean, and the only prints on it are yours."

"It gets worse," I said.

"What?"

"My mother said the police removed a white pill bottle from the bedroom area. She saw them carry it out in a clear plastic bag."

"Oh, wonderful," she said, shaking her head in disbelief. "You realize this implicates you, Becky. If the contents of the pill bottle match the tox screen, you immediately become a suspect, at a minimum."

"But I was in New York! How could I be a suspect?"

"Co-conspirator, perhaps?"

My blood boiled a little at that point. "Are you saying you don't believe me, Rachel?"

"That's not the point, Becky. What I believe doesn't matter. It's what the police, the prosecutor, and potentially, the jury believe."

"Do you think they'll arrest me?"

"Probably," said Rachel.

"What about my mother?"

"Maybe."

"Shouldn't we tell her about the pills?"

"No."

"Why?"

"Let me try to get ahead of this, Becky, please."

"How?"

"I'm going to try to meet with the prosecutor who heads up the homicide division."

"You're going to tell him about the pills?" I couldn't believe it.

"Becky, they know about the pills! They seized them, remember. I need to tell the prosecutor that you saw them just before your month-long trip to New York and had no idea where they came from. Bottom line: it looks like you're being framed again, Becky."

CHAPTER 18

I T WAS FRIDAY, and Rachel told me she'd get back to me by the end of the day. She didn't expect an arrest that day, but said it could happen over the weekend. I needed to figure something out that might help me, so I tapped into my recently acquired investigative reporter mode, recalling Tilly's three words: *Who would know?*

I thought about who had been in my house recently. My parents had been there, of course, but I doubted either of them would put an unmarked bottle of Xanax pills in my medicine cabinet. To my knowledge, neither took any pills like that. They medicated only with alcohol, as far as I knew. Ruling them out, I asked myself who had been in the house during the weeks before my departure to New York. No work had been done, so no plumbers, electricians, or other tradespeople were required at the house. Since my release from jail last summer, I'd purposely avoided having guests. I felt safer that way. That left the maids.

Like many residents of Paradise Valley, I used a

maid service that came to clean once a week. The company I chose was called Juanita's Maids. They would send two to four people to clean the house, and they could usually finish everything within a couple of hours. Rusty and I would let them in and either run errands or take a long walk along the canal while they worked in my home. It would be easy for one of them to place the bottle in my medicine cabinet, drawing no attention to themselves. The maids always split up and handled different areas of the house individually, so one would not be aware of what the other was doing at any given time. The issue was that the maid service didn't send the same people each week, and I didn't know any of them, not even their first names. I was never home when the maids were there except to let them in, and they were always gone by the time I returned. So how would I find out who to even ask about the bottle?

I figured the best way to start was to call the office of Juanita's Maid Service. I didn't like what I was about to do, but since my freedom was at stake, again, I did it. The cell phones back in 2005 didn't have nearly as much storage capacity as the ones today, but there was enough memory to save several contacts on the phone. Since I called Juanita's often because of conflicts in my schedule with their service times, I had that phone number in my phone's contact list. I dialed the number and waited for someone to answer.

"Juanita's Maids," came a woman's voice with a Hispanic accent.

"Hello, this is Rebecca Moreland, on North Thirty-sixth Place."

"Yes, ma'am. How may I help you?"

"I'm sorry to tell you that an expensive piece of jewelry is missing from my home. I'm worried that one of your people might have stolen it."

"This never happens with our company. We hire only honest people."

"I'm sure you try. Are you saying no one has ever called you with a problem like this before?"

"Sometimes people call, but our workers never take anything."

"I understand. But if you work with me, we can solve this problem easily."

"Okay. What do you want?"

"I'd like to speak with everyone who cleaned my house in January."

"Hmmm. Well, we have a list of them, for sure. Let me look at the computer right now."

I waited while the woman typed on her computer. I assumed I was speaking to the company's owner, likely Juanita herself, since she had the authority to handle the situation without involving anyone else. So far, so good. She returned to the call. "Five different people came to your house for cleaning in January," she said.

"Are they all still working there?"

"All but one."

"What is her name and address?"

"I'm not supposed to give that out."

"I don't believe there's any law against that. What is your name, by the way?"

"Juanita. I own this company."

"Well, I'm glad I'm speaking to the owner because this was a very valuable piece of jewelry. I would hate to have to call the police on this."

"So if I give you the person's name and address, you won't call the police, even if you find nothing from her, right?"

"Yes, that's right. I promise."

Hesitation, then capitulation. "Her name is Rose Mendez. She lives at 114 West McDowell Road, Apartment Nine, Phoenix, Arizona."

"Thank you, Juanita. You're a lifesaver."

CHAPTER 19

I RECOGNIZE THAT SOME of you might think I was taking a significant risk by speaking to just one of the five maids who had been in my home in January. If she hadn't done it, I would come up empty. Those of you with a legal background will also understand the risk I faced in calling Juanita's. That could haunt me in various ways if I were accused of this crime—witness tampering, suspicion of using the maids for my own ends, or even paying them to commit the crime. But at that moment, it didn't matter to me. I had taken risks before, and they had paid off.

Now, Rachel was trying to meet with the prosecutor in the homicide division, which I regarded as highly unlikely to succeed. I believed the prosecutor would view my admission of having seen the pills, yet done nothing about them, much like a dog looks at raw meat. There was no way he would believe my excuse of not having time, not being concerned about the pills, or merely putting it off until later. My view was that no one was going to get me out of that mess except myself. Rachel was helpful, but limited in ways that I wasn't. So, I proceeded with my plan.

I'll share my theory upfront. I believed Rick had made his way back into the country, returned to Phoenix, and staked out my house. He identified my maids and followed one of them home. Then he bribed her to plant the pills in my medicine cabinet. Based on what I knew about Rick, if he were going to bribe anyone, it would be a substantial amount—enough for a mother with young children at home to take some time off from work. If you're wondering where Rick would get the money, I had no doubt that he'd been putting money offshore for a long time, even before he devised his scheme to murder my husband. This theory was the basis for my latest "Hail Mary" scheme. And here is where it led me:

It was 4 p.m. on Friday afternoon. I parked my car in the lot of a Food City grocery store across the street from where Rose Mendez lived. McDowell was a large, busy street near downtown Phoenix, filled with sketchy shops, eateries, and rundown apartment complexes. I crossed the street at a traffic light and made my way to 114 McDowell. Maria lived on the second floor of the dilapidated apartment complex. I went up the outdoor stairway, approached number "9," and knocked. After a few moments, a muffled voice came from inside. "Quien es?" ("Who is it?")

I spoke loudly so she could hear through the door. "Soy Rebecca Moreland. Trabajabas para Juanita, no?" ("It's Rebecca Moreland. You used to work for Juanita, right?")

I'll translate the rest of the conversation into English for you.

"Why do you want to know?" asked the woman behind the door.

"Because she sent me to you. I might be able to help you."

"I don't need any help!"

"I think you do. I can help you stay safe."

"Safe from who?"

"From the man who gave you the money."

I heard a chain lock unlatch, and the door opened. A frightened-looking woman in her twenties with long, dark hair stood before me. "Come in," she said. I stepped inside, and she quickly closed the door behind me, locking the chain. The room had a worn sofa and a few plastic chairs. The carpet was torn and dirty, and the smell of fried food lingered in the air. "Why do you think I'm in danger?" she asked.

"The man who gave you the money is a dangerous man, Rose. He is wanted for murder."

"Why would he hurt me?"

"He needs to make sure no one can tie him to his latest crime."

"What did he do?"

"He killed my father with the pills he asked you to put in my medicine cabinet."

Rose raised her hand to her mouth and drew in a sharp breath. "Oh my God! I didn't know!"

"I know, Rose. I know. And I can help you."

"How?"

"I know a lawyer who can help you. I'd like you to meet her."

"She can't protect me here! He knows where I live. He followed me home."

"And then he gave you the money to help him, right?" She nodded. "What did he tell you to do, Rose? Tell me everything you remember."

"He gave me a plastic bag with a bottle in it. He told me not to open the bag until I was at your medicine cabinet. He said to wear my rubber cleaning gloves when I took the bottle out of the bag, then put the bottle in the medicine cabinet. When I finished, I was to throw the empty bag away."

"When did you do it? What day did you put the pills in the medicine cabinet?"

Rose got up and walked into the kitchen, and I followed her. She glanced at a calendar mounted on the wall that had writing on it. "It was Thursday, January 27."

That was three days before I left for New York. I wondered if Rick knew that or if it was merely a coincidence. Had he placed the pills there to scare me, to show me he was back in town and coming for me? Or did he know my plans—that I was leaving and my parents were coming to stay at my house? I thought I knew the answer to that, but at that moment, I had more questions for Rose. "How much did he give you?"

"Ten thousand dollars."

I figured Rick would pay too much. She probably would have done it for a thousand, maybe less. "What did he look like?"

"He was tall and thin, with long dark hair and a beard."

The tall and thin sounded right, but Rick never kept his hair long and never sported facial hair. It made sense, however, that he would do that to disguise himself. How could I find out for sure if it was him? Then it hit me. "Was he wearing sunglasses?

"Yes."

"What did they look like?"

"I don't know, exactly. But they were different."

"How were they different, Rose?"

"They had one long lens for both eyes. Not one for each eye. And they had a word on the sides. It began with a 'P.'"

PRADA. Yep, it was him. "Okay, Rose. Look, this guy is dangerous. You need to get a new apartment, okay? Somewhere not near here."

"But my family lives nearby. My mother helps watch the children."

"I understand. Can your mother move with you?"

"Maybe."

"All right, listen to me, Rose. And listen carefully. I need you to tell the lawyer I mentioned what you told me. If you do that, she and I can help you make sure you and your family stay safe."

"How can you do that?"

"I have money, Rose. More money than the wicked man. I'll make sure you and your mother can move to a friendly neighborhood where you'll be safe."

"When?"

"Soon, Rose. There's no danger right now. Just stay inside with your door locked, like you've been doing. Do you have a phone here?"

"Yes."

"Please provide me with your phone number. I will call you when the lawyer is ready to speak with you."

Rose gave me her phone number, and I left the apartment. There was one more person I needed to see.

CHAPTER 20

I DROVE TO KATLIN'S house in Paradise Valley. An old Chevrolet sedan with Arizona plates sat in the driveway. I parked beside it and walked up to the front door. Katlin answered, greeting me with a smile that felt a little forced. Her two children—four-year-old Ricky and three-year-old Ashley—stood beside her. Buster, the Golden Doodle, lingered at the back of the foyer, wagging his tail with hesitation. Seeing the kids softened my heart considerably; I hoped they were too young to fully understand what was happening in their lives right then. If their dad had returned, perhaps for a brief visit, only to leave quickly, they must have had questions. Each of them smiled back when I greeted them. I turned my attention to Katlin, who hadn't invited me inside. "I need to talk to you for a moment, Katlin. Privately."

"I'm always happy to speak with you, Becky, but I was on my way out just now." Her voice seemed strained in a way I hadn't heard before.

"Whose car is that in the driveway?" I asked,

wondering if it could be Rick himself. Not likely. He wasn't that foolish, or was he?

Katlin responded forcefully, as though she wanted me to leave. Now. "That belongs to the sitter. Like I said, I need to head out."

"This will take five minutes, Katlin. After all I've done for you, you owe it to me."

"All right," she said, moving inside. "Please wait here, and I'll have the sitter watch the kids while we talk." Katlin led the kids out of the room and returned to speak with me in the foyer. She seemed determined to keep me out of the main body of the house. "What can I do for you, Becky?"

"Have you heard my father died?" I asked.

"Yes. I'm so sorry. Was it sudden?"

"It was murder."

She raised her eyebrows, surprised. "What? How could that happen?"

"The same way it happened to Peter. An overdose of Xanax dissolved into his Scotch."

"Oh my, that's just awful, Becky. I'm so sorry."

"Katlin, have you seen Rick lately?"

Again, surprise. Or was it fear? "Of course not. He's been gone for a long time. You know that." She seemed defensive.

"Yes, he has," I said.

"So what are you saying, Becky?" she asked, perturbed.

I considered how much I should tell Katlin, deciding to keep it minimal. If she was in touch with Rick, the less she knew, the better. However, I needed more than her body language and tone to confirm my suspicions. Before I left for New York, I informed Katlin about my trip and mentioned that my parents would stay at my house while I was away. If she had told Rick, he would have realized that an opportunity for revenge lay before him. Was he really that vindictive? Couldn't he see that all the terrible things that happened were his fault? Then it struck me—of course, he couldn't. He was a narcissist on steroids. I'm sure there was a medical term for his condition, but it meant that someone like Rick could never take responsibility for their actions. He would always shift the blame onto others. In this case, he blamed me for separating him from his family, for his kids having to grow up without a father, and for Katlin being alone without a husband. And he was going to get his revenge if I didn't stop him.

All these thoughts raced through my mind, prompting me to reconsider my perspective. I shouldn't view Katlin as Rick's co-conspirator; rather, I should see her as another one of his victims. I changed my mind about what to say to her. "I wanted to say, I'm sorry, Katlin. I'm sorry for what you and the kids are going through."

She softened, and then her face contorted. She

collapsed into my arms and squeezed me tightly. I felt the tears on her face as she pressed her mouth to my ears. "Help me!" she whispered.

I pulled my head back, still holding onto her. "Is he here?" I said, softly.

She nodded, fear in her eyes.

"Okay, listen to me." My voice was barely audible. "Tell him you got rid of me and that I just came to check on you. You'll be fine, Katlin. You and the kids will be okay." She nodded again, and I pulled away from her, raising my voice. "All right, it's good to see you. Let's get together soon, okay?"

I left the house, ran to my car, and quickly backed out of the driveway. Then I thought I should get the license plate of the car in the driveway since it was probably being driven by Rick. I slammed on my brakes and pulled back in. I took a pad and pencil out of my purse and wrote down the license plate from the beat-up old Chevy. Then, I backed out again and drove away. I quickly took my phone out of my purse and called 9-1-1. The operator answered the phone on the second ring. "Nine-one-one. What is your emergency?"

"My friend Katlin and her two kids are being held in her home by a dangerous intruder."

"What is the address?"

I gave her the address.

"How many people are in the home?"

"My friend Katlin, her two children, ages three and four, and the intruder. He's there and she's scared."

"Are there firearms in the home?"

"I don't know, but the man is dangerous. He's a murderer, a fugitive, and extremely dangerous."

"What is his name?"

"Rick Miller."

"I have someone on the way, ma'am, but I need more information."

"Okay, fine. Just tell the cops to be careful. This man is dangerous."

"I realize that, ma'am. I need a description of the intruder. What is his race?"

"White."

"Height and weight?"

"He's tall and thin."

"Can you be more specific?"

"He's about six feet two and one hundred eighty pounds."

"Facial hair? Tattoos? Other identifiers?"

"I was told he grew a beard and let his hair grow long. And he often wears expensive PRADA sunglasses."

"What is your name, ma'am?"

"My name is Rebecca Moreland."

"What is your location? Are you safe?"

"I'm driving my car. I'm nearly at my destination."

"What is your address?"

I gave her my mother's address.

"Lock your doors and wait there. Officers will contact you. Is there anything else?"

I remembered the car. "Yes, there was an old Chevrolet sedan parked in the driveway. I wrote down its license plate."

"What is the plate number?"

I gave it to her and as much of a description of the car as I could remember.

"Anything else, ma'am."

"No. Please help her!"

"We are responding. Standby at your mother's house. Units are on the way."

The 9-1-1 operator hung up the phone.

CHAPTER 21

WITHIN MINUTES, I arrived at my mother's home. She met me at the door and asked what I'd been up to. I asked her to give me a minute and called Rachel on her cell phone.

"This is Rachel," she said.

"It's Becky. There's a lot going on. I need to speak with you urgently."

"Okay. I have some things to go over with you, too."

"That can wait. Let me bring you up to speed."

I told her about my meetings with Rose Mendez and Katlin Miller. Things got really serious at that point.

"Has Rick Miller been arrested?" asked Rachel.

"I don't know," I said.

"Then you need to get out of the area immediately," she said.

"I'm at my mother's. It's a gated and guarded community, and the security system is top-notch."

"Listen to me, Becky. You and your mother need to get out of there right now. Go up into the mountains.

Maybe Flagstaff, Sedona, or Prescott. Get a hotel and call me when you arrive."

"What about Rusty?"

"The dog?"

"Yes."

"Bring him with you. There are plenty of dog-friendly hotels in those towns. Do this now, Becky. I'll try to find out what happened at the Miller residence, but that will take time. Call me when you're settled. We'll talk then."

I hung up the phone and brought my mother up to date, telling her we would have to leave immediately. My bag was still packed since I hadn't touched it since returning from New York earlier that day. My mother put a few things together, and we piled into my car, putting Rusty in the back seat. We took Tatum Road to Cactus and got on the 51, then took the 101 to Route 17 North, the interstate that went up into the mountains on the way to Northern Arizona. We went to Sedona and stayed at the El Portal, one of the most dog-friendly inns in the country. Peter and I had stayed there with Rusty before, and he loved it. I called ahead and got a room.

When we were safely in our room, it was nearly 8 p.m. Before I called Rachel, I called Katlin Miller.

"Miller residence," she answered.

"It's Becky. Are you okay?"

"Yes." Her voice was stiff.

"Did they arrest Rick?"

"No, he got away. The police are here. They want to know who I'm talking to."

"You can tell them. I just want to know you're safe."

There was a pause, and I heard Katlin telling the police it was me. Then she came back onto the line. "They want to know where you are, Becky."

"I can't tell you that, Katlin. Not with Rick on the loose. I advise you to take the kids and Buster and get out of town."

"The police aren't going to let me do that."

"Then tell them to move you somewhere. They need to protect you."

"I'll try," said Katlin, exasperation in her voice.

"Listen, Katlin. Do you know an attorney you can call for advice?"

"Yes."

"Tell the police you want to speak to your attorney. That will get them to become more cooperative."

"Okay."

"What's important is that you're safe right now. But you need to get somewhere that Rick can't find you, okay?"

"I don't think he would hurt us, but the kids are so confused. I don't see a good ending to this, Becky."

"Call the attorney."

"I will," said Katlin.

"Great. I've got to go and do that very thing myself. Be safe, Katlin."

"You too."

I hung up the phone and called Rachel. I told her that Rick Miller had gotten away, and she sighed, then admonished me. "Becky, how many times have I begged you not to talk to anyone about the case? You're making my job so much harder!"

"But I've only been home for eight hours, and I already flushed Rick out!"

"And he's on the run and probably looking for you. How does that help us?"

"I have proof that it was him! Why can't you hear that?"

"I do hear that, Becky. The problem is you've made yourself into a witness by inserting yourself into the investigation."

"Why is that a problem? There's no case against me. Rose Mendez will testify that she was paid to put the pills in the cabinet by a man resembling Rick Miller. Katlin Miller will confirm that Rick is here! So, I'm happy to be a witness in his trial when he's caught. But there won't be a trial for me. There's no case."

Rachel was having none of my presumptuous interpretation of where things stood. "You are the most stubborn, obstinate client I've ever had. And while you actually do get results, your methods may still come back to haunt you. Yes, you found Rose Mendez, and yes, she told you things, but have you thought about what will happen if Rose Mendez goes missing or is otherwise unavailable to testify? Then what?"

"What about Katlin Miller?"

"Just because her fugitive husband stopped by for a visit proves nothing. The strongest case remains against you, especially without Rose Mendez."

"Then go get her! Hide her. I've already told her I'd give her money for a new apartment!"

"WHAT??? You're kidding me. You've just tampered with a key witness. You're a train wreck, Becky. And your arrogance doesn't even let you see it."

I took a deep breath, trying to hear what Rachel was saying. "Okay, what do we do now?"

"You stay where you are and don't do anything else. Just relax and spend some time with your mom and your dog, and leave it to me."

"What are you going to do?"

"I'm going to do this the right way, Becky."

"What happened with the prosecutor today?"

"Nothing, yet. But now I have a lot more to work with. And yes, it came from you, but enough is enough. Give me Rose Mendez's address. That's all I need, and my investigator will take over our witness interviews. Meanwhile, I'll speak with the prosecutor again and update you. But you need to stand down and give me some time to work. Okay?"

"Okay."

"I'll talk to you over the weekend," said Rachel. "Goodbye."

"Bye."

I hung up the phone and turned to my mother. "Well, that didn't go as well as I hoped it would. But she told me to relax so I'm going to follow her advice. Why don't we get something to eat."

CHAPTER 22

THE COUNTY MEDICAL examiner released my father's body to the funeral home on Saturday. My mom and I worked together on the arrangements. He was a well-known and respected man in the community, so we expected a large crowd. His services and burial would occur the following Friday.

On Saturday afternoon, Tilly called my cell phone. "How are you holding up?" she asked.

I felt sincerity in her tone, but she undoubtedly wanted to discuss more than that. "I'm doing fine. I'm with my mom and my dog, Rusty."

"I imagine there's a lot going on for you right now," she said. "There's quite a bit of chatter coming out of Phoenix about your father's death."

"I'm sure there is. But I can't talk to you about it, Tilly. You've probably heard enough to know why."

"I understand. You realize we'll put somebody on the story to cover it, right?"

"Yeah, sure," I said. "By the way, do I still have a job?"

"Oh yes. Take what time you need to sort this out, and we'll get you goin' when things settle down for you. Just don't end up in jail again, okay?"

I wanted to tell Tilly I was innocent again, but resisted the urge. Rachel would be happy about that. "Thanks for calling, Tilly. I'll let you know when I see light at the end of the tunnel, okay?"

"You got it, Becky. Stay strong, girl."

On Sunday, Rachel called. She told me the car Rick had been driving had been found at the airport, meaning he'd probably escaped by air again. Rachel said the police would review CCTV footage to identify which flight he'd taken, enabling them to discover what alias he was using. Police traced the car back to an owner in the Maryvale section of town. It might have belonged to one of Rick's relatives, so the police were following up on that lead.

"What happened with Rose Mendez?" I asked.

"My investigator met with her, and her story was consistent with what she told you."

"Is she safe? Did you find her a safe place to stay?"

"That's not how this works, Becky. It's part of what I'll cover with the prosecutor first thing tomorrow morning."

"But she's in danger! I thought you were going to talk to the prosecutor right away?"

"First, it's highly likely that Rick Miller has left the area since we found the car at the airport. Second, it's the weekend, Becky. I called the prosecutor's office and left a message that I needed to speak with him urgently. But Maricopa is a big county, and it was a busy weekend for homicide. Your father's case is just one of many. But I assure you, I'll get in there and speak with him tomorrow."

"Do you have time to explain what you hope to achieve with the prosecutor?" I asked.

"Several things, actually," said Rachel. "But everything will hinge on my investigator's taped interview with Rose Mendez. I'll play it for the prosecutor, then ask him for what is known as a 'Queen for a Day' agreement."

"What's that?"

"Officially, it's called a proffer agreement. It means that Rose can provide information to the prosecutor regarding the crime while limiting the prosecutor's use of the information against her. In other words, Rose will be protected from prosecution to a considerable degree, even though she was involved in the crime."

"What about keeping her safe?"

"A lot of pieces have to come together for the prosecutor to offer protection for Rose. First, he has to agree that her statement is relevant. I think he will. Then he needs to corroborate her story with other relevant evidence, such as CCTV footage of Rick parking near her apartment, walking down the sidewalk, or finding other witnesses who saw a person of his description in the area when Rose says he visited."

This didn't make much sense to me. "But finding more evidence seems difficult. And it will take time. What if Rick flew to LA and is returning here now? He'll go straight to Rose's apartment and kill her! I'll pay for her new apartment. Just get her safe. You told me she was our key witness, and we needed to protect her."

"And that's what I'm working on, Becky. You cannot be involved in this. What you've done already is a problem. Paying for Rose to get a new apartment looks like a bribe. That would definitely make things worse. I assure you that everything I can do to protect Rose is being done."

I didn't respond immediately. The whole legal process was so frustrating to me—it had been the first time around, too, and it was again. I breathed an enormous sigh that Rachel had undoubtedly heard over the phone.

"Becky, try to be objective for a minute. What if *you were* the perpetrator? What if you'd tracked Rose Mendez down, given her money to tell the story, the very story she's telling us right now? That's why independent corroborating evidence is needed. We need something to make the prosecutor confident you didn't set this whole thing up. Does this make sense to you?

Now I understood. "Yeah, it does make sense. I wish you'd told me that from the beginning."

I heard a sigh from Rachel's end of the line. "Becky,

it's all about you letting the investigation unfold. And that applies to everything that happens from this moment forward. Can I count on you to do that, or do I need to withdraw from representing you?"

Wow, Rachel had said nothing like that to me before. All along, I thought I was helping, and I had, but I'd also caused a lot of headaches for her. I really needed to control my impulses. I'd had considerable success when taking matters into my own hands, but I didn't want to gamble with my life by losing an attorney I trusted who was one of the best in town. "I'll follow your instructions, Rachel. I promise."

"Good," she said. "I'll reach out to you tomorrow."

CHAPTER 23

A

S EXPECTED, INVESTIGATORS found only my fingerprints on the Xanax bottle. Everything depended on Rachel's meeting with the prosecutor. That was the only thing preventing my arrest at that point, aside from the fact that no one knew where I was, including Rachel. The prosecutor was willing to delay issuing an arrest warrant while his team searched for corroborating evidence. Rachel's investigator was also working on that.

After six days in Sedona, my mother, Rusty, and I returned to Phoenix for my father's funeral. It was a somber affair because news of his murder had spread. Not only that, but several people seemed to think I was responsible. Some glared at me, while others turned away as I approached. Overall, the proceedings did little to ease the grief I felt from the loss of my father. Surprisingly, my mother was the one who helped me through it.

The service ended, and the crowd dispersed, leaving my mother and me alone at the grave. "May I stay with you and Rusty for a while?" she asked, reaching for my hand.

"Of course, Mom. That would be nice."

My home was no longer an active crime scene. Police removed the tape, and we were free to return. I had to figure out where to go. We could stay at my home, go to my mother's, or retreat back up into the mountains and keep hiding. I didn't like the idea of hiding. I needed to move on with my life, and I had a job that I was eager to pursue. So, I decided to stay in Phoenix, at my home.

I drove my mother to her place, and Rusty greeted us. She packed a few things while I called a security company and arranged to have more cameras around my home and property. They suggested that I run sensors along the perimeter of the wall surrounding our backyard and the gate itself and I agreed. I also called a contractor to replace the door in my house with the dog door cut into it. All of that would happen in a matter of days.

With my home secured as much as I could make it, I went to buy a gun. The gun shop owner ran the background check and glanced up at me while reviewing the information. I had been a convicted felon not long ago, but had been vindicated in December 2004. But apparently, that wasn't enough to allow me to buy a gun.

"I'm sorry, ma'am, but the background check indicates you're a convicted felon. I can't sell you a gun."

"But I was found innocent last December."

"I can also see that information, ma'am, and I know who you are. You're pretty famous." The man smiled, trying to make me feel better, I guess. "Still, federal law prohibits any person convicted of a felony from owning a gun. Even if you were later found innocent."

"Wow, that doesn't seem fair," I said, disappointed and wondering how I would protect myself and my mother from Rick if he were to break into my home.

"I'm sorry ma'am. I followed your case closely, and I believed in your innocence from the outset. But I hope you respect that I'm a law-abiding citizen and that I run my business accordingly."

"Yes, of course, Mr...?"

"Watkins. Sam Watkins."

"Thank you, Mr. Watkins." And then it came to me. "By the way, my mother is in need of a gun. Can she buy one here?"

"If she passes the background check, sure," said Mr. Watkins.

Problem solved. "She's trying to protect herself from a potential intruder."

"I understand, Ms. Moreland, and she has a right to do that because of the Second Amendment. I wouldn't have gone into this business if I didn't believe that with all my heart."

"What kind of handgun would be appropriate for an older woman to use to stop an intruder?" I asked.

Mr. Watkins thought about my question. "I'd rec-ommend the EZ version of the Smith and Wesson M & P Shield. It's a lightweight nine-millimeter that's easy to rack and has mild recoil. It's got an eight-round cartridge that's easy to load. It's a true beginner's gun and was designed for women. But you should tell your mom to practice at a gun range, no matter what gun she buys."

"Thank you, Mr. Watkins. Can you recommend a gun range for my mom?"

"We've got one here. And we give lessons."

"Are you allowed to give lessons to someone like me, even though I'm not permitted to own a firearm?"

"I'm sorry, ma'am, but no. The federal statute pro-hibits possession or use of a gun by a convicted felon."

"I understand. Thank you for being so helpful, Mr. Watkins. You may be seeing my mother in the near future."

"Of course, Ms. Moreland. Tell her to make sure to ask for the 'EZ.' Otherwise, she might end up with a Smith and Wesson that's more gun than she can handle. By the way, I'm a big fan of yours. I hope you stay safe and happy."

"Thank you. Oh, one other thing. I've taken a job as an investigative reporter. Would you be available to answer questions if I ever encounter situations involv-ing guns?"

"I'd be happy to help however I can, ma'am."

I sent my mother to buy the gun from Mr. Watkins, giving her a piece of paper with the model number on it. She purchased the gun along with several ammunition cartridges and brought them home. I read the operating instructions for the weapon and practiced using it without a cartridge. Then, I placed it in my bedside table drawer and forgot about it. Little did I know, I would soon need it.

CHAPTER 24

Late monday evening, Rachel called with news about her meeting with the prosecutor. He'd found Rose Mendez's statement relevant, especially since Rick had been at Katlin Miller's home recently, and her description of his appearance matched Rose's description. The search for other corroborating evidence would continue, but the prosecutor was inclined to believe that I hadn't influenced Rose, even though I had gone to see her.

"So, am I cleared of any wrongdoing?" I asked.

"No, but you're not going to be arrested at this point."

"What about Rose? Is he going to protect her?"

"Not yet, but I think he's close. If we could get just one more piece of corroborating evidence, I think he'll seek a protective order for Rose Mendez."

"What's a protective order?"

"It's an order from a judge barring Rick from coming near Rose Mendez."

"That's worthless," I said, getting angry.

"Yes, but we can hope that enough corroborating evidence comes along to get the prosecutor to do more for her."

"We should just tell her to move. Now. She's got the money, after all."

"I'm afraid she doesn't," said Rachel. "Whatever money she had left from Rick's bribe has been seized. She can't profit from a crime, Becky."

"Wow, this just goes from bad to worse. My key witness, who needs to be protected for me to stay out of jail, not only isn't being protected, she's unemployed and has no money. This is bullshit, Rachel!"

"I'm sorry, Becky, but this is how the system works."

"Can you please tell her to relocate?"

"Relocation has already been suggested, and Rose has been advised to provide any address change to the prosecutor's office."

I was fed up. For the first time, I questioned whether Rachel was the right attorney for me. She had led me to believe that Rose would be protected if I let her handle it, but now she was essentially telling me that Rose was in a dire situation. On the other hand, it was clear to me now that the word "protection" meant something in the legal world that it didn't mean in the world the rest of us lived in. I would give Rachel the benefit of the doubt. She had always had my best interests at heart, and let's face it, Rose Mendez wasn't her client. She would protect her to the degree the law allowed, if for nothing else than to protect me.

"Are you staying in town, Becky?" asked Rachel. "I heard you were at your father's funeral."

"Yes, I'm back at my home. My mom is with me."

"I'd recommend getting an alarm expert there to ensure you've beefed up your security to the maximum extent possible."

"One step ahead of you. They'll be here tomorrow to do the work. So will the contractor who'll be putting in a steel door to replace the one with the dog door in it."

"Great. Good work."

"How long do you think the investigation for corroborating evidence will take?" I asked.

"First, there's no certainty that any evidence will be found. I'd say that every avenue of inquiry will have been tried in a week or two. Hopefully, something will turn up."

"I hope so," I said, but I wasn't happy about waiting another two weeks until Rose could be protected. That Rachel lacked confidence that anything would be found was also discouraging.

"I recommend you just lie low right now, Becky. Are you able to do that?"

"I'll do my best," I said, but I already knew that was a lie.

As soon as I finished with Rachel, I called Katlin

Miller. When she answered, I asked her how she was doing. "I'm scared and confused," she said. "I don't know what to do. The police say I should stay here and call them if Rick shows up again, but I don't want him to show up again. I don't want to see him ever again! He's a murderer, and I don't want my kids ever to know that. I just want to leave town and go somewhere he can't find us. Maybe even change our names."

"What does your attorney say?"

"He says I should cooperate with the police."

"Hmmm. At least you don't think Rick would hurt you."

There was a pause. I didn't like that pause. Something was going on with Katlin that was very disturbing. Before she responded, I made a suggestion. "Say, why don't we meet for coffee tomorrow morning, Katlin? We can talk more freely that way."

"Sure!" she said, almost as if this was precisely what she hoped would happen. "I'll drop the kids at my parents' and meet you at Hava Java on Thirty-second and Camelback. What time is good for you?"

"How about eight o'clock?" I asked.

"Great! See you then!"

"Katlin, you're safe right now, right?"

"Yes, I am. I'm fine, Becky. I just need someone to talk to."

"Okay, great! I'll see you in the morning."

CHAPTER 25

BEFORE I LEFT the house to meet Katlin for coffee, something inside me urged me to bring the gun. Perhaps it was because I was meeting with Katlin. Rick was obviously in contact with her, which was an opportunity to catch him, but it also presented him with a chance to catch me. I went to the bedside table, pulled out the gun and a cartridge, and inserted the cartridge into the gun. I looked at the instruction booklet to double-check where the safety was and made sure it was on. I stuffed the gun in my purse and left the house.

I parked out front in the crowded lot serving the Safeway store, a hair salon, and various restaurants. Katlin was waiting for me at Hava Java. It was cold that morning, so she'd secured a table in the cramped interior rather than sitting outside, where the tables were further apart. The table was a two-seater stuffed into the corner, so at least there was some level of privacy. The noise of conversation in the room would also help cover up our voices.

Katlin stood as I approached and hugged me tightly. "Why don't you hold our table while I get our coffees," she said. "What would you like?"

"Just a regular, black," I said.

Katlin left to get in the line, which was long but always moved quickly. She returned with two coffees and two muffins. "I thought you might be hungry," she said. "We've got a blueberry muffin and coffee cake."

I smiled and pulled the coffee cake toward me. "Thank you."

Katlin sat down and sipped from her coffee. She looked nervous, and I wondered if it was because she had a lot to tell me or something else.

"I thought it would be best to talk in person," I said. "You seem like you have a lot going on and might need a sympathetic ear."

"You are so right," she said. "There's a lot going on."

I nodded my head slowly and smiled. I didn't want to give the impression that I was desperate to learn more, but inside, I was chomping at the bit for her to get on with it.

Katlin reached into her purse and pulled out a cheap-looking cell phone. She spoke quietly. "He gave me this."

"Hmmm. What does he want you to do with it?"

"He wants me to always keep it with me and wait for his call. When he calls the next time, he'll give me instructions on what to do next."

"What do you think he wants you to do?"

"I know what he wants. He wants us to run away with him. He said he would give me instructions on where to meet up with him the next time he calls. He's been living in a place that has no extradition agreement with the United States. He claims he could get us all new IDs with new names. He said the kids could keep their first names and are so young they wouldn't even know their last name had been changed, that they wouldn't even remember our old lives here. That it was the perfect time for a change like this."

"Did he give you a number where you can call him? To report on what's going on. Like if the police come and ask questions. Stuff like that?"

She nodded. "I already called him once to tell him what the police asked me the day you called nine-one-one for me."

This threw me for a loop. "Are you trying to help him?" I asked.

She quickly shook her head. "No! But he specifically asked me to call him when he ran out of there to get away. He wanted to know what the police asked when they came to the house."

"How did he know to run? Why did he suspect the police might be coming?"

She hesitated, her mouth turning down in a frown. "I told him I thought you were suspicious and might call them."

"Why?"

"I wanted him out of there!" she hissed. "If he'd been there when the police arrived, he might have held us hostage or something."

"Katlin, did you tell the police everything you're telling me now?"

She frowned again. Clearly, she hadn't.

"What about your attorney?"

She shook her head.

"Why?"

"I'm confused!" she said.

I realized Katlin had loved Rick and might still love him. She had asked for my help, and I felt her request was genuine. Perhaps all she needed was a nudge in the right direction from me. But before I could decide which way to push, I had to learn more.

"How long have you had that prepaid cell phone, Katlin?" I asked.

"A while," she said.

"So Rick has been to see you more than once since he disappeared last June?"

She nodded.

"When was the first time he visited?"

"In December."

"Do you remember the date?"

She shook her head. "It was around a week before Christmas. I don't remember the exact day. He brought

Christmas presents for all of us. The kids were confused. They didn't even recognize him."

"When did he give you the burner phone?"

"That first time. He told me he would call me to check on me. That I should keep him informed if anything of interest happened."

"Did you call him to tell him about my new job when I told you about it?"

She nodded.

That explained how he could time the planting of the Xanax bottle so precisely. "Did he say anything about what happened to Peter or my father?"

"He said he'd had nothing to do with either of their deaths."

"Do you believe him?"

She shook her head firmly.

"So why are you helping him, Katlin?"

"I feel like he knows what's going on in my life. Like he'll know if I'm working with the police."

"Do you think he's watching you?"

"Kind of. I can't explain it, but sometimes he knows where I've been. Like when I go to the grocery store, sometimes he'll call and ask me how the shopping went. But when I ask him how he knew I went shopping, he just says it was a good guess."

I had to decide right then and there if I could trust Katlin. She was obviously conflicted, and while she said she didn't think Rick would hurt her, I wasn't sure she truly believed that. She was seeking help, looking for guidance, and she was looking to me to provide it. Given what had happened to Rose Mendez, I was hesitant to recommend that she go to the police with all she knew. After all, Rose had done the right thing. She made a statement to the investigator and was cooperating with the police, but all she received in return was an offer to reduce her sentencing for her role in my father's murder. Yet, she still wasn't being protected by the police, and they took all the money she received from Peter. Katlin's situation was different, but would the police treat her any better than they had Rose Mendez? I would have to think about that.

I decided to trust her. "Hey, I understand the confusion you're having, Katlin. And if I could be so bold, maybe you *are* a little worried that Rick might do something to you if you don't cooperate. Are you?"

She nodded meekly, tears welling up in her eyes.

"Katlin, listen to me. Withholding all of this evidence from the police has probably put you in really hot water. But you might limit the damage by giving it to them now. You'll need to speak to your lawyer about the best way to handle this, but you should do that as soon as possible, okay?"

She had a distressed look on her face. "I'm scared," she said.

"I know, I know," I said, reaching out and taking

her hand in mine. "What needs to happen is that you should get your kids safe first. Where are they now?"

"They're at my parent's house."

"Okay, when you leave here, I want you to go to your parents' house and tell them you need their help. Don't give them any details. Just tell them you think the kids are in danger and they need to take them out of town. Have them go to the mountains—either Flag or Prescott or Sedona. And make sure they don't tell you where they're going. They can communicate with you by cell phone."

"Why can't they tell me where they're going?"

"Because you might tell Rick. That's why."

"I won't tell him!"

I put out my hand, palm up. "I know, I know. But maybe he'll force you to."

She understood what that meant, and she didn't attempt to refute it.

"After you know your kids are safe, you go to your attorney and tell him everything. He'll figure out the best approach to use with the police. Can you do all of that, Katlin?"

She nodded.

"I need to hear you say it."

"Yes!"

"Okay, what will you do with all of this information?" she asked.

"I honestly don't know, Katlin. But I promise I'll

give you time to get your kids safe and meet with your attorney. After that, I'll probably disclose all of this to my attorney. I just have to think about it."

"Okay," she said. "But Becky. You need to be careful too. Rick blames you for all of this."

"I know he does. And that alone should tell you how messed up his mind is."

She nodded. "Becky, what if he followed me here this morning?"

Whoa! That was a shocker. I hadn't considered that. How would the two of us get out of here if he was out there, lurking in the parking lot? "Where did you park?" I asked.

"Behind the Collins restaurant. There's always parking spaces there."

That was because the back of the Collins was the back of the entire storefront. Not nearly as busy as the main lot in front, where I had parked. "I'll walk you to your car," I said.

As we left Hava Java, I reached into my purse and discretely pulled out the Smith & Wesson handgun, putting it in my jacket pocket and keeping my finger on the trigger.

CHAPTER 26

K ATLIN AND I left Hava Java together and walked across the parking lot toward The Collins Small Batch Kitchen. As we strolled along the side of the restaurant toward the back parking lot, I slipped my left arm through Katlin's. Arm in arm, we rounded the corner. Katlin drove a large white Ford Expedition, presumably to fit her kids and their friends. When I spotted the car parked alongside the back of the brick building, I noticed a tall man with long bleach-blond hair leaning against it. He was clean-shaven, but it was clear it was Rick. He still wore those fancy Prada sunglasses.

When he saw me, he reached into his pocket, but I jerked my gun out first and pointed it at him. "Don't do it, Rick!" I yelled. "I'll shoot you where you stand." And I wasn't kidding. There stood the man who had murdered my husband and my father. I wanted to kill him. My blood boiled in a way that I hadn't felt before. I would pull the trigger if he kept reaching for his gun.

Rick raised his hands and suddenly decided to run.

I pulled the trigger, but nothing happened—the safety was still on. Rick dashed along the back of the long building and vanished around a corner. I turned to Katlin, who appeared to be in shock. "It's going to be okay, Katlin. Get in your car and head to your parents' house. Have them leave town with the kids and not tell you where they're going. Then go to your attorney and share everything you told me. Don't go home, understand? Check into a hotel where Rick wouldn't expect you to be and stay there. Call me when you can."

She nodded.

"Tell me everything you're going to do, Katlin."

She repeated my instructions back to me. I hugged her and went to find my car. By the time I reached it, I was still shaking with adrenaline. I drove home, parked in the garage, and entered the house. I updated my mother on the situation, told her I thought we'd need to leave town again, and asked her to pack a bag. While my mom was packing, I called Rachel and was stunned by what she told me. "Rose Mendez is dead."

Anger and guilt competed for attention inside me. I was furious that the system had let this happen and guilty that I'd ever involved poor Rose in this tragedy. And frankly, I wasn't happy with Rachel either. "I told you we should have had her move! But oh no, that wasn't your job. No, I was your client, not Rose. And you told me to stay away from her, even after the police stripped her of the only money she had!"

"I understand how you feel," Rachel said. "I feel that way sometimes, too. Of course, we sympathize with Rose Mendez, but we can't forget that she accepted ten grand to do something she shouldn't have. I also understand your frustrations. However, I signed up to work within this system, and I do my best. If you don't believe I've been acting in your best interests, I'm willing to refer you to another attorney. But honestly, Becky, I'm not sure how many reputable attorneys would want to represent you. You're a loose cannon, and that's the last type of client any reasonable attorney wants."

Rachel's words had calmed me somewhat and helped me think more clearly. There was too much happening for me to search for another attorney, and much of what Rachel had said resonated with me. "So, why are you keeping me?" I asked.

"I don't really know, Becky. Probably because I care about you, and I know you didn't commit the crimes you've been accused of or suspected of."

"What will happen with my case now that my key witness is dead?"

"Honestly, it may help with your case. We have Rose's statement preserved. It's admissible in court. It's obvious that you had no incentive to harm her. She was critical to your case. Rick, on the other hand, the prime suspect in your husband's murder and your father's murder, had every reason to harm her and now will become the prime suspect in her murder. That's three murders pointing at him."

"So I'm off the hook? Is that what you're saying?"

"Very likely, unless you've done something else you haven't told me."

Well, yes, I had done something else that very morning, and I had to decide how much to tell Rachel about what had happened. If I was going to continue with her as my attorney, I needed to share something, if not everything, but she'd probably quit when I did that. It was a no-win situation for me. I started my confession. "Rachel, there is something else."

"Oh, great!" she said, the sound of her exhaling audible over the phone.

"I know, believe me. I know exactly how you feel."

"And how would you know that?"

"Because I've been advising someone who's worse than me."

"What are you talking about?"

"It's Katlin Miller."

"You're telling me you've been talking to Katlin Miller?"

"I have, and while I think my information would be really helpful to everyone involved, including the police, I'm afraid it might upset you very much."

"Oh, just bring it on, Becky."

I told her everything that Katlin had told me and described the encounter with Rick, but I left out the fact that I'd had a gun. Rachel knew there was some missing information.

"So what do you think would have caused Rick Miller to run? After all, you said you thought he had a gun. Did you or Katlin have a firearm in your possession?"

"Let me ask you this, Rachel. Would it be better for you *not* to know the answer to that question?"

"That depends on whether the answer is a "yes" or a "no." If it were "Yes, I did have a gun, and I pointed it at him, then that would be bad.""

"Rachel, I can only say this. I'm alone, unprotected, and vulnerable. There's a three-time murderer on the loose who wants to kill me. Some might say it would be a good idea for me to have a gun. But since we both know I'm a convicted felon, I cannot possess a gun."

"We can end this hypothetical now, Becky. Let's move on. By the way, did you or Katlin call the police to alert them that a fugitive and suspected murderer was on the loose in the Safeway parking lot?"

"Well, uh, no. I didn't even think of that. Plus, I thought I told you Katlin has a whole host of her own problems regarding withholding information from the police."

"I'm not worried about Katlin's problems, Becky."

"I told you I didn't think of it, Rachel. I should have. What are you going to do with the information I just gave you? Am I fired? Or are you going to help solve this case?"

"Regarding you being fired, I need some time before deciding on that. But if you want to fire me, I encourage you to do it right now. Regarding the information from Katlin and the events of this morning, I could probably keep it quiet by relying on attorney-client privilege. After all, you're the one who provided the information. But I don't think I should sit on it. People, including you, are in danger, and the police need to catch this guy. But if I go forward with the information, they will want to talk to you, and they will be looking at CCTV footage and seeking witnesses. Do you understand that this might bring up fresh problems for you? I don't think it will affect any of the pending murder cases, but remember, I don't know everything you know. Having said all of this, do you want me to go forward to the police?"

"Absolutely. But what about my safety? I think I should leave town again."

"You probably should. I can explain to the police that you fear for your life and are seeking shelter elsewhere."

"Do you want to know where I'm going?"

"Yes, this time I do."

"I'll be at El Portal in Sedona. With my mother and Rusty."

CHAPTER 27

I DIDN'T GO TO Sedona. I would have, except things didn't turn out that way. Because I hadn't heard from Katlin, I called her and was surprised by her new attitude. "My lawyer says I'm not supposed to speak with anyone about my case," she said.

"Yeah, that's what mine says, too. But I've always come through for you, Katlin, even though you were at the top of my attorney's 'No-No List.'"

That softened her up a bit. "Thanks for this morning," she said. "But Rick sure wasn't happy about me meeting with you. He called that phone he gave me and interrogated me about our get-together. I told him I was trying to find out what you and your attorneys were up to. That calmed him down, but he was disappointed when I told him you wouldn't tell me anything. I said all you wanted to do was find out if the kids and I were okay."

"So you called your attorney?"

"I did. He and I went to the police to report the incident with Rick and to make them aware of everything

I didn't tell them during the first interview. They're not going to charge me for withholding evidence, but they want me to help them catch Rick."

"What do they want you to do?"

"They asked me to keep them informed when he calls and try to set up a meeting with him where they can apprehend him. It's all kind of frightening."

"I hear you. You did the right thing, though. Say, did you mention to the police that I had a gun on me this morning?"

"Why yes, I did. I thought I should be forthcoming about everything. Is that a problem for you?"

"It's the truth, so no worries. I'll deal with it."

"We probably shouldn't speak anymore, Becky. Until this whole thing is over."

"You're right, Katlin. You be safe, okay?"

"You too."

Not long after I hung up with Katlin, Rachel called. She had news about my status as her client. "I've met with my partners, and while you've made many mistakes, we're going to stick with you, primarily because of the imminent threat to your well-being. However, there are some conditions."

"Like what?"

"It goes without saying that you discuss nothing about any of the active cases with anyone other than me."

"I can do that," I said. "I will do that."

"Thank you. The other thing is that if there is a firearm that you have access to, you need to surrender it to the police. If you know the owner, they need to come with you to the police. I'll be there too, and the gun owner should also bring their attorney."

Hearing this, I was glad I'd spoken to Katlin before Rachel called. She'd told me the police knew I had a gun, so I was already in trouble for that. But I didn't know how much trouble. "It's my mother's gun," I said. "What will happen to us if we do what you ask?"

"In your case, you'll be charged as a prohibited possessor of a firearm. It's a Class Four Felony, which can carry up to four years in prison."

"You're kidding me! It was self-defense!"

"Doesn't matter. You shouldn't have possessed the gun, Becky. But listen, I'm confident we can plead it down to a lesser charge, which should result in no jail time and one-year of probation."

"What about my mom?"

"She could be charged."

"With what?" She didn't do anything!"

"She provided a weapon to a prohibited possessor. That's a Class Four Felony as well."

"She didn't even know that I took the gun out of the house. She's innocent!"

"Calm down, Becky. I don't think your mom will be charged, assuming her record's clean. Worse case, she does probation, same as you will be."

"What does probation entail?" I asked.

"The good news is that if your probation goes off without a hitch, the felony will be reduced to a misdemeanor. You have to report to the probation officer after your sentencing. The probation officer has a lot of leeway in how often you report to them and what you have to do. But at a minimum, they expect you to remain employed and law-abiding and to report any contact with law enforcement."

"What about my job? Will they even want to employ me if I'm a convicted felon?"

"It's treated as a felony conviction until your successful completion of probation, but I don't know your company's policies in that regard."

"Can I speak to them about it?"

"Of course, but knowing who you work for, I'd counsel you to say as little as possible."

"Got it. I'll speak to my employer and my mom and get back to. Is there anything else, Rachel?"

"You tell me."

"Nothing to report. But I do have one more question. Does probation mean my travel is limited?"

"Yes, it does. You'll have to give up your passport and won't be able to leave the state during your probation without the permission of your probation officer."

This was too much. "You realize I'm being hunted by a murderer, right? I can't protect myself with a gun, and I can't relocate. I'd say I'll be dead before the year is over."

"I disagree," said Rachel. "Maricopa County is the largest county in the country, geographically. You can get a short-term rental in North Scottsdale and Rick could never find you. And just so you know, pepper spray isn't classified as a firearm, and there are pepper spray guns that can disable a pursuer from a long distance. Plus, you're a woman of means. If you want to hire a bodyguard, you are free to do so. You can protect yourself from Rick Miller, whether you're on probation or not."

"Thanks Rachel. That's actually very useful information. I wish you'd told me all of this sooner."

"Well, you're still here, so I guess that's water under the bridge. Let me know your decision regarding my firm's conditions of representation soon, okay? If you want to stay with us, we'll want to run down to the police with the gun sooner rather than later."

"I'll call you by tomorrow if that's okay."

"That's fine, Becky. Have a good evening."

CHAPTER 28

I SPOKE TO MY mom about what Rachel wanted us to do with the gun, and she was fine with it. My mother had changed so much since my father passed away that I hadn't even recognized it. She had become kinder and more affectionate. For my entire life, she had supposedly been allergic to dogs, but now she loved Rusty as much as I did, showing no signs of allergy symptoms whatsoever. She treated me with respect and warmth—a touch to my arm here, a brief hug there, and a compassionate smile when I was feeling down or scared.

"I think it makes sense," she said. "If I'm honest, I relish the idea that I might become a convicted felon. I realize that's a foolish thing to wish for, and it's not like I've been looking to become a criminal. But in some bizarre way, it will be a badge of honor for me. We're fighting for our very lives, and we've done something that some might say is foolish because we've broken the law. But the gun very well saved your life today, Becky. And for that, I'd sacrifice anything. You and Rusty are all I have left, you see." She sucked in a ragged breath and wiped away a tear.

I was touched. My mom was becoming...my mom. I can't say I agreed that I liked the idea of being convicted of a felony, but I appreciated her affection toward me. Her love for me. "Well, Mom, like I said, Rachel doesn't think you'll be charged. But there's always hope!" We laughed together and decided to have a glass of wine.

At around 8 p.m., Phoenix time, I called Tilly. New York was two hours ahead that time of year, making it ten there, which was early in the City. "Tilly Blankenship," she answered.

I heard voices and soft music in the background. "Hi Tilly, it's Becky Moreland. It sounds like I've caught you out."

"No, it's fine, Becky. I'll step away from the table. Just having a nightcap with an old friend." After a few seconds, Tilly continued. "I've been wondering how you're doing down in the Valley of the Sun. How can I help you, honey?"

"Well, I wanted to update you, off the record, if it's okay."

"Sure," she said. "I'm all ears."

I tried to keep things simple. "My father's death has been determined to have been an overdose of benzodiazepine."

"Xanax again," she said. "I'm so sorry, Becky."

"Thank you, Tilly. It was a shock, but I'm not a suspect."

"You were here in New York, for goodness' sake. Why would you be a suspect?"

"Some complicating factors could have led people to the wrong conclusion, but Rick Miller is the primary suspect."

"So he's back?"

"He's back. And that's the main reason I'm calling. I felt I was in danger from Rick, so I had my mother buy a gun. You know I can't possess a gun because of my original murder conviction, right? Even though I was later found innocent."

"Yeah, I know that stupid law. It's come up before in some of the stories we've reported on over the years."

"I agree it's a stupid law, but I got in trouble because of it. I actually scared Rick off with the gun. I didn't fire it, but I had it in my possession. And the police know about it."

"Ooops. So what happened?"

"It hasn't happened yet, but my lawyer says the right thing to do is to surrender the gun to the police. I'll very likely be charged with prohibited possession of a firearm. It's a Class Four Felony. My lawyer says she can plead it down to a lesser charge, with no jail and a year's probation. And after that, the conviction will probably be reduced to a misdemeanor."

Tilly didn't take long to figure out where I was

going with this. "So you want to know how the company will feel about employing a convicted felon."

"Yeah."

"The fact is that we're already employing a convicted felon, right? You've said so yourself."

"Yeah, that's technically true. But this is a new charge, and it happened while I was an employee."

"Right," she said, thinking. "I suppose I should run this by legal on Monday, but as far as I'm concerned, you did what you had to do to protect yourself."

"Thanks, Tilly. You're a good friend."

"Did they catch Rick Miller?" she asked.

"Not yet. But they're working on it. I think they'll either catch him, or he'll bolt for good. He's not a very smart criminal."

"So few of them are," said Tilly, chuckling. "You be careful, okay."

I hung up the phone and considered what it would mean to wait until Monday to turn myself in and surrender the gun. I had told Rachel I'd have an answer for her tomorrow, on Saturday. The more I reflected on it, the more I understood it didn't matter what my employer had said. Sure, I wanted the job, but I didn't need it to survive. The courts would surely understand that I was independently wealthy and didn't need to work. Regardless, I felt a powerful compulsion to set things straight and keep Rachel as my attorney.

The next morning, I called Rachel and told her

that my mother and I were prepared to surrender the gun to the police. She mentioned it could wait until Monday, which would give her better access to the prosecutor's office to negotiate a plea deal. She expressed her thanks that I was coming forward with the gun and reminded me that I should look into some of the more potent pepper spray options.

I spent the rest of the weekend searching for short-term rentals in North Scottsdale and looking for the pepper spray guns Rachel had mentioned. Finding dog-friendly places narrowed down the options significantly, but we identified a few that accepted dogs and went to check them out. One of them seemed decent, so we rented it for a month. On the way home, I stopped at a sporting goods store and concluded that a canister of bear spray would be just as effective as a pepper spray gun. It could disable an attacker from twenty feet away and was seriously powerful. Peter and I carried bear spray when we camped in Wyoming a few years back. If it could stop a bear, I figured it could handle Rick Miller.

On my way home from North Scottsdale, my cell phone rang. It was the alarm company. My house had been broken into, and the police had been dispatched. When we arrived, three police cruisers with flashing lights were in front of my home. Typically, there would have been one or two at most, but Paradise Valley PD was familiar with my home due to all that had happened there in recent years. So three police cars didn't surprise me. Thankfully, no reporters had arrived yet. I parked the car on the side of the road and approached an officer standing beside his squad car. "I'm the homeowner, Rebecca Moreland. What's happening?"

"I'm sorry to say your home was broken into, ma'am. The guy climbed over the back wall and broke a window in the kitchen. He couldn't have been in there long, because he got away."

"Was there any damage?"

"Quite a bit, ma'am, but it's worse. He hurt your dog."

"Oh, my God! He's not dead, is he?"

"No, ma'am. He was conscious when we arrived, and he seemed more scared than anything. One of our officers took him to the twenty-four-hour vet. I think he's going to be okay."

CHAPTER 29

I ASKED THE POLICE what vet they had taken Rusty to, and my mom and I hurried over there. They led us straight to the room where they were caring for Rusty. He was awake but had a large bandage wrapped around his head. The vet explained Rusty had been struck in the head with a blunt object. It had opened up a wound that they had sewn up. He was on antibiotics and painkillers. They told us they wanted to keep him overnight for observation, and I agreed, assuring them I would be back first thing in the morning to pick him up. I was concerned that Rusty didn't react as we backed out of the room, suggesting that he was so out of it he couldn't recognize who we were. This worried me, but I had other pressing problems I needed to deal with. The vet was the right place for Rusty at that moment. They would take better care of him in his current condition than I ever could.

We returned to my home. Once the police finished dusting for prints, they allowed us to enter the house. My mom didn't want to go in, so I left her in the car and went inside. The kitchen was a wreck. Most of my dishes and glassware were now shattered on the counters and floor. Fortunately, only the kitchen sustained damage. I would call someone to clean up the mess.

I didn't want to leave my mother alone in the car for long, so I quickly surveyed the rest of the house. I noticed footprints going up the stairs. There had been a little blood on the kitchen floor, probably Rusty's, and the intruder must have stepped in it while it was still wet. I followed the prints up the stairs. They led into the master bedroom but were fading away by the time I reached there. My first instinct was to check on the gun, which I had put back in the drawer of my bedside table. I opened the drawer. No gun. He'd taken it. *Crap!*

I reset the alarm and returned to my car. One police cruiser remained, and an officer stepped out to speak with me. "We'll inform you of the results of the prints, Ms. Moreland. I'm really sorry this happened."

"Thank you, officer."

"I'd get that window fixed as soon as possible, ma'am."

"Yes, I'll call someone soon," I said.

I got into my car and noticed my mother was quietly weeping. I reached over and held her hand. "We'll be okay, Mom. I promise."

"I don't want to stay here," she said.

"Neither do I. I'll go in and pack some things, and we can go to your house until Monday.

I went back inside and packed for both of us. While packing, the thought crossed my mind that I might never spend another night in that house. Our rental in North Scottsdale didn't start until Monday, so we drove to my mother's home on Camelback Mountain. I called a cleaning service, explained the job that needed to be done, and they said they could meet me at my house in a few hours. Next, I called a handyman I had used before who worked on weekends, and he said he could come over Sunday to take measurements for the window. He was sure he couldn't get the new window that same day, but he knew of a boarding-up service that could come and board up the window while we waited for the new one to be delivered. All I had to do then was call Rachel.

I told her about the break-in, Rusty's injuries, and the theft of the gun. Rachel expressed her condolences and then got down to business. She explained we could still go through with the plan to turn ourselves in for the gun violation. She asked if my mother had kept the bill of sale, and I confirmed she had. Rachel told me to bring it when we went to the police on Monday morning. "I'm so sorry this is happening to you, Becky. You need to find another place to stay until Rick is caught."

"Been there, done that, Rachel. The rental starts on Monday. We've got it for a month right now, and I'm sure we can find another one if we need to stay away longer. Honestly, I think I'm going to put my home up for sale. There's just been too much bad that's happened there."

"I understand," she said. "Did you get a pepper spray gun?"

"Bear spray," I said.

"That should work. I hope you don't have to use it. I expect you won't now that you've found a discreet place to stay."

"Thanks, Rachel. We'll see you Monday morning at Paradise Valley PD."

"No, it's not Paradise Valley PD for the gun. It's Phoenix PD, since you were in Phoenix when you committed the crime."

"Oh, okay. Can you email the address?"

"Sure thing. See you soon."

The hard part came next. I asked my mom if she was okay with being alone while I went for a walk. I explained that I'd meet the clean-up people at my home after the walk. She nodded, still not talking much. I didn't want to leave her, but I had to go. I grabbed the bear spray and drove down to the canal where Rusty and I walked every day. I parked my car, went onto the canal path, and started walking.

Conflicting emotions boiled inside me I had to sort out. I was so angry at Rick. I'm ashamed to admit it, but at that moment, I honestly wanted to kill him more than ever. I chastised myself for leaving the safety on the first time I'd had a chance to shoot him.

He hurt Rusty because of my incompetence. I also felt frustrated that I couldn't own a gun and would never be allowed to learn how to use one. We wouldn't be afraid to stay in my home if I'd at least disabled him, so he couldn't run. I could have shot him in the leg, and he'd be behind bars now. If anyone needed the protection of the Second Amendment, it was me. But they had relegated me to pepper spray and bear spray as my primary defense against an unhinged murdering lunatic.

Despite all the conflicting emotions, I forced myself to calm down, trying to connect with the part of myself I had always relied on in the past— the part that guided me on what I needed to do. Steps turned into miles, and I lost track of time as I walked along the canal. I had brought no water and was thirsty, but I kept going. Soon, I would reach the crossing at 44th Street. There were some shops there where I could get some water. I felt so drained of energy that I finally let go and reached the place in my mind where I wanted to be—my inner self. It told me that turning ourselves in on Monday was the right thing to do. Then it allowed me to see that I already possessed all the knowledge I needed to find Rick Miller.

CHAPTER 30

LATE SATURDAY AFTERNOON, I brought home Chinese takeout for dinner to share with my mom. We ate together, but my attention wandered. I wanted to reflect more on what I knew that could lead me to Rick. My mom noticed. "What's on your mind, dear? You seem a bit distant right now."

"I'm sorry. I was thinking about how we might catch Rick Miller."

She raised her eyebrows. "I hope you don't mean that we hunt him down and blast him with bear spray. After all, he has a gun. We no longer do."

"No, nothing like that. I'm going to play by the rules this time. But that doesn't mean I can't use my mind to help with the investigation."

"I like that approach," she said. "You do seem well-suited to your new career."

"If it doesn't get dead-ended before it even starts," I lamented.

"Something tells me your career will be just fine," she said.

"I hope so."

"Why don't I leave you alone to think for a while? You can use the Quiet Room."

"Thanks, Mom. I think I'll do that."

After dinner, my mother went to watch the news. I poured myself a glass of wine and went to the Quiet Room, settling into one of the comfortable chairs. I took a long sip of wine, trying to relax, and I succeeded. Suddenly, the clue I had been trying to remember came to me. When Katlin and I had coffee at Hava Java, she said, "I can't explain it, but sometimes he knows where I've been." How could Rick know that? Was he staking out her house and following her? Was that even realistic? I didn't think so. After all, it was an exclusive neighborhood. Many part-timers only came in the winter, but no one left their house empty all year. And very few rented them out. Plus, it *was* winter, when everyone wanted to be in Phoenix. Any home near enough to see Katlin's had an occupant. That line of thought seemed like a dead end.

Then I had another thought: what if he could track her car? I went to my luggage and pulled out my IBM ThinkPad. I was pretty good with computers, and I'd made sure my mom and dad got Wi-Fi service years earlier. I even knew their password since I had set up the router for them. Neither of them went online much, but I often did when I was there. And that's exactly what I did then. After a quick trip to the kitchen to refill my wine, I settled back in my chair, booted up my laptop, and went to work. I searched for "GPS tracking devices for cars" and was surprised to find that a local spyware shop was a place where civilians could buy them. Further research showed me a picture of what they looked like: little rectangular boxes about the size of a pack of cigarettes. Some versions could be placed inside vehicles, while a few could be mounted on the outside.

I was excited, thinking that maybe Rick had put one of those on Katlin's car. I resisted the urge to call and ask her to check her car. I wasn't going to do that anymore. I was going to do it Rachel's way; at least, I was going to try. Then another epiphany hit me. What if Rick had placed a tracker on my car? He could have done it the very morning Katlin and I were having lunch at Hava Java. I decided to try and find out.

Because it had gotten dark and my car was parked in my mom's driveway, I borrowed a flashlight from her. I stepped outside, and it didn't take long to find the tracker hidden under my front bumper. He'd gone to the trouble of drilling through the bottom of the bumper and attaching a case for the tracker with screws. He must have brought a rechargeable drill with him. He'd planned the whole thing carefully. Then I realized he knew where I was, even at that moment! I left the tracker in place and rushed inside to call Rachel.

"Rachel Cohen," she answered.

"Hi, it's me, your favorite client."

Rachel chuckled. "Is everything okay?"

"Just peachy," I joked. "I just found the GPS tracker that Rick attached to my car."

"Oh, crap!" she gasped. "I hadn't thought of that."

"And he's probably got one on Katlin's car as well. That's how he tracked us to Hava Java that morning."

"And he probably knows you went to North Scottsdale. He may have even followed you there, so I'd say cross that destination off your list."

"Agreed. What should we do now?"

"I'm going to send my investigator out to your mom's place right now, if that's okay. You didn't remove the tracker, did you?"

"No, I didn't. What's he going to do?"

"He's going to confirm that it's what you think it is. While he does that, I'll contact the Paradise Valley PD. We might be able to turn this to our advantage."

"Absolutely. And don't forget about Katlin. Perhaps you should call her attorney and let him know what I found."

"I'll let the police do that, Becky. And don't get any ideas about doing it yourself. This all needs to be coordinated by the police."

"Okay. What should I do now?"

"Wait for my investigator to get there. His name is Karl Kaminski. And keep that bear spray nearby. If

Rick Miller knows where you are, he might show up, too. I'll get back to you when I know more. Karl will be there with you for a while. Don't worry."

I hung up with Rachel and went to inform my mom about what was happening. It was going to be a long night.

CHAPTER 31

KARL KAMINSKI CAME over and confirmed that the device attached to the inside of my front bumper was indeed a GPS tracker. He left shortly after that, and my mother and I went to bed.

We picked up Rusty early Sunday morning. He was happy to see us and seemed much more alert than before. The vet provided some pain medication and suggested scheduling an appointment with our regular vet in ten days to have the stitches removed. Unfortunately, they had to put a cone on Rusty to prevent him from scratching his wound until the stitches came out. This caused issues for us from the start, including getting him into the car. He couldn't jump into the back seat like he usually did, so we had to lift and push on his rear until he was finally inside. He bumped the cone against the backs of the front seats while trying to get comfortable, but eventually settled down, sitting in the middle of the back seat where he wouldn't have to deal with the two front seats anymore.

After we had Rusty home and settled, things got

complicated. Rachel called and said the police were moving quickly regarding a plan to capture Rick. They had confirmed that he'd also placed a tracker on Katlin's car. They wanted to meet with Katlin and me to discuss their ideas for ensnaring Rick in an ambush.

"Isn't it risky for us to drive down to police headquarters with Rick tracking us?" I asked.

"Yes," Rachel said. "That's why I'm picking you up. Katlin's parents will take her and the kids, as if they were on a Sunday family outing. They'll drop Katlin off at Paradise Valley PD and keep the kids with them until this is all over."

"Wait. What? When do they want to do this?"

"Tonight."

We met with the police. The plan was for me to drive over to Katlin's that evening. Rick would know I was there because of the tracker. He wouldn't like it, especially if I stayed for more than a brief visit, which was part of the plan. I would remain there until he arrived, even if it took until the early hours of the morning. There would be two plainclothes police officers inside the house and one walking the neighborhood, posing as a dog walker. The two inside would park far away in unmarked cars and walk into the neighborhood on foot, then enter through Katlin's front door separately. They would approach the house after it got dark, around 6:30 p.m. I was to drive over to Katlin's at 7:30 p.m.

I was fully committed to the plan, but I wondered why Katlin was so eager to agree to it. After all, she had two young children and was their only parent. Rick couldn't be counted on to help them at all, considering he would either spend the rest of his life in prison—likely on death row—or escape again to whatever exotic place he'd settled in overseas. When I asked her about it, her response made sense. "I want this to be over, Becky. The stress this is causing me is unbearable. Heaven forbid something happens to me during this manhunt—or whatever you want to call it—but you know, who's to say Rick won't turn on me anyway? He's a killer and completely unhinged. I'll take this option any day over letting this drag on for who knows how long."

With the plan in place, Katlin's attorney drove her to her parents' house. They planned to drive her home later in the afternoon but keep the kids. Rachel drove me home. During the ride, I asked her, "What about our plan to turn ourselves in for the gun violation tomorrow?"

"Since the gun violation is Phoenix PD, we can still proceed. They won't be involved in tonight's sting, but if we succeed, they might view you more favorably for your help in catching a wanted murderer. The more victims Rick kills, the higher he climbs on the Most Wanted List. Phoenix PD is well aware of Rick Miller, especially since one of his alleged murders occurred in their jurisdiction. But let's not dwell on that right now, Becky. Let's focus on getting through tonight first."

Rachel dropped me off at my mom's home and wished me luck. She seemed nervous for me, and I appreciated her concern. But I wasn't worried. I wanted Rick Miller captured more than anyone. I brought my mother up to date, and she suggested we have a drink to calm our nerves. I declined. I wanted to have all my wits at my disposal for the evening activities.

CHAPTER 32

A T 7:15 P.M., I slipped the bear spray into my purse and headed to Katlin's house. I wasn't sure if the police would want me to have the bear spray during the operation, but I didn't plan on showing it to them. While I didn't expect to use it, if it came down to it, I would spray that bastard with every ounce of what was in that bottle.

I arrived at Katlin's house, parked in the driveway, walked to the front door, and knocked. Katlin let me in and took me to the back of the house. There were two police officers there, but before they could even introduce themselves, Katlin's burner phone started ringing.

One of the police officers said, "Put it on speaker. Everyone except Ms. Miller keep really quiet."

Katlin nodded. Everyone held their breath while Katlin answered the phone.

Rick's voice came through the speaker. "Step away from her and go to a part of the house where she can't hear you."

"Give me a second." Katlin didn't move but waited a few seconds, then spoke into the phone. "Okay, I'm in the bedroom."

"What the hell is she doing there?"

"Who?"

"That bitch Becky Moreland! She wants to kill me, you know."

"I don't think that's true, honey. By the way, how did you know Becky's here?"

"That doesn't matter. Tell her to leave."

Katlin looked at the police officer for directions. He held up his index finger and mimed the pressing of a button while mouthing the word "Mute." Katlin pushed the mute button on the phone, and the officer provided direction. "Tell him she came over to keep you company while the kids are doing a sleepover."

Katlin pushed the mute button again and told Rick what the officer had told her to say.

"That's bullshit! Why are you being friendly with her?"

"I don't know, Rick. I just like her."

Rick severed the connection, and silence ruled the room.

"Listen up," said the lead cop. "This might be it. You ladies sit over there on the sofa. I'll be right over here in the dining room, and Cristo will guard the front door." The cop named Cristo gave me a reassuring smile. His brown eyes sparkled with sincerity, and I felt a spark of something else. Was it attraction? He was a handsome man of Hispanic descent, around thirty and over six feet tall, dressed in a brown sweater and khaki pants. He left the room and headed toward the foyer at the front of the house.

The lead cop grabbed his walkie-talkie and spoke to the dog walker, advising him to stay alert because the suspect might be approaching. Then he moved to the dining room to hide. I took the bear spray out of my purse and removed the pin that prevented accidental spraying. This time, I wasn't going to let a safety hold me back from firing.

The next thing I heard was a deafening gunshot in the dining room. A body fell, and Rick stepped into sight at the entrance to the dining room. Now he was bald, and for once, he wasn't wearing those hideous Prada sunglasses. I raised the bear spray and pulled the trigger. The stream of foul poison hit him right in the eyes. I kept spraying, my heart beating fast, and I'm ashamed to say, enjoying what I was doing to him.

"Ahhh!" he screamed, dropping his gun and bringing both of his hands to his face. The other police officer, Cristo, was on him then and had no trouble dropping him to the floor and cuffing him.

Rick moaned and writhed while Cristo called for backup. The dog-walking cop was soon pounding on the front door and Katlin went to let him in. Cristo yanked Rick from the floor, his arms handcuffed behind his back. The bear spray had temporarily blinded him, his face red and swelling, head down and lolling from side to side. But he knew we were there. "I did it all for you and the kids!" he yelled. "All I wanted was a good life together, Katlin! I love you!" His agonizing cries sounded like a wounded animal. It was eerie, and I could see that Katlin was deeply shaken.

The police escorted Rick out of the house. They had captured him, but another person was dead. The officer in the dining room didn't make it.

CHAPTER 33

RICK HAD BEEN living in the pool house in the backyard of Katlin's home. It was a fully functional cottage, allowing him to keep the lights on in the back without them shining through the windows facing the house. Microwavable meals and plenty of beer filled the refrigerator. He could enter the home through the kitchen door using his own key. Katlin had never changed the locks, and I wondered how that had slipped through the cracks.

On Monday morning, my mother and I went to Phoenix PD, accompanied by Rachel and my mom's attorney. I turned myself in for illegal possession of a firearm, and we handed over the gun registration certificate, informing the Phoenix police the gun had been stolen during a home invasion, likely by Rick. I found it disconcerting that the Paradise Valley police had not recovered my mom's gun from the pool house in Katlin's backyard. It was still missing.

Here's the thing, though: The Phoenix Police didn't charge my mom, and they didn't charge me.

A cop died in the line of duty, and I probably saved another officer's life (the one named Cristo) by using the bear spray. I almost certainly saved my own life, and maybe Katlin's, too. At the very least, I helped capture a multiple murderer. No one was pressing charges against me that day for a crime that mattered little in the total scheme of things. Word traveled quickly in the law enforcement community, and the Phoenix PD undoubtedly knew what had happened in Paradise Valley the previous evening.

I spoke to Rachel about giving my employer an exclusive on the Rick Miller case. She promised that I would be cleared of any involvement in the murders and free to talk within a week. But she reminded me I had been part of a large team that resolved this mess and that I should respect the police and their role in bringing Rick into custody. As I reflect on that moment, it gave me a greater appreciation for Rachel's perception of her role in the criminal justice system. She was an important part, but so were the police, and she was asking me as an investigative reporter to honor their sacrifice. That wouldn't be hard for me. I'd witnessed the ultimate sacrifice by one of their own.

A week later, I called Tilly and offered her my story. She said it would serve as a great launching pad for what she expected to be an outstanding career in journalism for me. The story received national attention, and my fame grew even more. Once things settled down, I immersed myself in the day-to-day aspects of my job as an investigative journalist. My mom sold her home and moved in with me and Rusty, and I couldn't have been happier. Over time, I entertained the idea of possibly meeting a nice man, but it wasn't a priority for me then. I wanted to focus on my work. While Tilly helped put the idea of assisting other innocent victims into perspective by noting that very few people suspected of crimes were innocent, I remained excited about being involved in high-profile cases full of intrigue. My own perilous journey lingered in my thoughts. I had to admit to myself that it had excited me in some fundamental way. I relished the thrill of being in jeopardy and using my wits to find a solution.

Katlin and I grew close after the ordeal we had endured at Rick's hands. The sale of my company occurred in March, and I wrote Katlin a check for two million dollars. I didn't need to, but I wanted to. Rick's craziness wasn't her fault. She had children to support and lacked the education or experience to earn a substantial income. After all, she was only twenty-six and had married Rick right out of college, having kids shortly thereafter. I wasn't sure if the money would be enough for her to remain in the large home in Paradise Valley, but it turned out she didn't really want to stay there anymore after what had happened. She sold the house and moved into a smaller, three-bedroom home in Biltmore Shores, just across 32nd Street from Paradise Valley.

My husband and father were dead. Rose Mendez was dead. A brave and dedicated cop was gone from this world. I had survived, and I truly appreciated it. I relished the chance to immerse myself in all the beautiful things that life could offer if I only sought them out. It seemed impossible then that I would ever face circumstances similar to what I had endured during the ordeal with Rick Miller. Things like that were so rare they could never intrude on a person's life more than once or twice, right? After all, a court wrongfully convicted me once, and it had almost happened again. I thought I was out of the woods based on the odds alone. But I was mistaken.

PART 3

CHAPTER 34

June 12, 2010/ Phoenix, Arizona

A S JUDGE MARIA Espinoza turned her head toward the jury, I was convinced they would find me guilty. Guards would escort me to the holding cell, move me to Estrella, and eventually transport me to Perryville, where I would serve out my life sentence.

The judge's voice burst through the silence in the courtroom. "Has the jury reached a verdict?"

The jury foreperson stood. He was an older, thin Black man in a gray suit and red tie, cleanly shaven. "We have, your honor." He grimaced a little as he said it, as if he didn't want the verdict to be what it was, but had no choice. The facts and evidence were what they were.

The jury selection process had taken longer this time than in my first two trials because I was still a bit of a local folk hero, having saved myself for a second time back when I'd hit Rick with bear spray. Time had passed, but my name had remained in the papers, this time as a journalist, publishing articles about cases I'd investigated. But all of that was about to come to an abrupt and final end.

"Please hand the verdict form to the bailiff," ordered the judge.

The bailiff approached the jury box, and the foreperson handed her the document. The bailiff walked the verdict form over to the bench and handed it up to the judge, who read the verdict to herself and then passed the paper to the clerk.

"Will the defendant please rise for the reading of the verdict," said the judge.

Rachel and I stood together. Had six years really passed since the first time we did this? I remember the reading of the verdict at my trial for Peter's murder vividly. My heart had been racing. But this time, I felt calm, resigned to my fate. Yes, I was innocent again, but the case against me was ironclad.

The clerk read the verdict. "On count one, murder in the first degree: guilty."

I nodded. To those watching, it must have seemed that I agreed with the verdict; that I had indeed murdered Cristo and acknowledged that I deserved what I had just received. Rachel touched my arm and looked at me with admonishing eyes. "Don't do that," she whispered, probably considering how it would look when she appealed the verdict.

The judge addressed the jury. "Is this your true verdict?"

All twelve jurors nodded and mouthed the word "Yes."

"Does either counsel wish to poll the jury?"

Rachel answered. "Yes, your honor."

The judge began the polling. "Juror number one, is this your true verdict?"

"Yes, your honor," said juror number one.

The judge continued, and all twelve jurors affirmed the guilty verdict. The trial was ending and so was my freedom.

"Thank you for serving on this jury," said the judge. "The admonition barring you from discussing this case with anyone other than your fellow jurors is now lifted. You are free to leave. Thank you for your service. All rise."

The gallery rose. The jurors stood and left the courtroom.

"You may be seated," said the judge. Everyone in the courtroom sat. Rachel gently pulled me into my seat. I was numb, depressed beyond measure.

The judge addressed the lawyers. "Are there any other matters before I set a sentencing date?"

"No, your honor," said the prosecutor.

"No, your honor," said Rachel.

The judge consulted with the clerk and then spoke. "It is ordered setting sentencing for August fifteenth at 8:30 a.m. in this division. A pre-sentence report shall be prepared and made available to counsel one week before sentencing. Sentencing memos are due at that time. Mrs. Moreland, I am now remanding you into the custody of the Maricopa County Sheriff's Office while you await your sentence. All bond is revoked. We are adjourned." The judge banged her gavel.

"All rise," said the bailiff. The gallery stood while the judge left the bench.

The sheriff's deputy, who had been present throughout the trial, approached the defendant's table, reaching for his handcuffs as he walked. "Please hold out your arms, wrists together, miss." His tone was gentle.

I turned to Rachel, who looked exhausted. She seemed older now, and the rings under her brown eyes were deeper and darker than the first time we had done this, her dark hair more disheveled. She smiled weakly and nodded, indicating that I should comply with the deputy's request. I extended my arms, and the deputy snapped on the handcuffs.

"I'll try to visit you tonight," said Rachel.

"It doesn't matter," I said. "You don't have to do that. I'll be okay."

They escorted me from the courtroom, and I galvanized myself for the long road ahead.

CHAPTER 35

March 2006

L ET ME TELL you how I'd been accused of murder again. And found guilty. Again. It all began the evening that we lured Rick into Katlin's home and caught him, in late-February of 2005. You may remember that the police officer who had captured Rick after I sprayed him with bear spray was a handsome man named Cristo. His full name was Cristo Perez.

Cristo and I met for the second time about a year after we apprehended Rick. Once again, it was perilous circumstances that brought us together. Since Rick's capture, I had worked as an investigative journalist. My alma mater, Arizona State University, had invited me to speak. It was an evening presentation at the Walter Cronkite School of Journalism, in early March of 2006. The topic was how I had adjusted from being an inexperienced novice—with no training other than my education at Cronkite and the one-month orientation I had completed in New York—to an investigative reporter regularly filing stories on white-collar crime, drug cartels, and serial killers, to name a few of the stories I'd covered during my first year on the job.

My speech was well attended. Most of the students had walked over from their dorms on campus. ASU was in downtown Phoenix, and some sections of the area were pretty rundown. At night, the area around the Cronkite School became eerily deserted. Most of the shops and businesses there shut down at around six.

After the speech, the auditorium emptied, but many students lingered and wanted to ask me questions. Several of them were looking for autographs.

Having ensured all the students were satisfied, I gathered my belongings and headed to the parking lot on Filmore Street. The lot was nearly empty when I walked out. I made my way to my car and got in quickly. Just as I was about to start the car, I saw a black panel van turn into the lot. The van stopped beside a lone young woman who'd been cutting across the parking lot. Before I knew it, the driver was out of the van. He was much bigger than the girl and easily controlled her. He pressed a handkerchief over her mouth with one hand and grabbed her around the waist with his free arm. Within seconds, he had shoved her into the back of the van and slid the door shut. He jumped into the driver's seat and the van slowly crept away. I was witnessing an abduction.

I'd gotten serious about martial arts after the troubles with Rick, but I didn't delude myself into thinking I could handle this guy physically. He'd looked like a very large and powerful man. I wasn't close enough, anyway. I called 9-1-1, and they asked the nature of my emergency. While I was answering the operator's questions, the van pulled casually out of the lot. I started my car and followed.

"Can you describe the vehicle?" asked the dispatcher.

"It's a black panel van. It looks pretty old."

The van turned right onto Central Avenue and headed toward Interstate 10, which went through Phoenix on the way to Los Angeles, a five or six-hour drive from town. If he went west on the Ten, the abductor could be in remote desert in minutes."

"Are the police on the way?" I asked.

"Yes, ma'am. Can you still see the vehicle?"

"Yes, I'm following, but if he gets on the highway Ten, it'll be really hard to stop him, won't it?"

"Our unit is closing, ma'am. Stay back."

Suddenly, I saw the lights of a police car approaching from the east on Roosevelt Street. The van had stopped at the traffic light where Central and Roosevelt intersected. The police car swerved and darted right in front of the van. A police officer jumped out, gun in his hands, and pointed it at the van. The van started backing up, its rear turning toward the curb.

There was no way I was letting him get away. I jammed my foot on the gas and roared up to the van, blocking his escape route. The window of the van rolled down and shots were fired. The passenger side window of my car exploded. I grabbed my purse, opened my door, and rolled out onto the street.

I pulled my pepper spray gun from my purse. I had stopped using bear spray and switched to an advanced pepper spray delivery system. I could shoot a pepper spray bullet that traveled up to fifty feet and would explode upon impact. The cloud it produced could disable an assailant even if it didn't hit them directly. I crouched down and heard more gunshots. Peeking around the front of my car, I saw the police officer face down on the ground. The guy from the van was getting out and looked like he might try to finish off the cop. I raised my pepper spray gun and aimed. He was only fifteen feet away. I pulled the trigger hard. The round hit him in the face and exploded. He went down, rubbing his face and eyes, squirming on the ground. I rushed over to the police officer. "Can you hear me?" I asked. He nodded. "Give me your cuffs."

The officer handed me his cuffs, and I rushed over to the perpetrator. I kicked him in the head but he tried to get up. I kicked him again. That did it. I slammed my knee into his back, pulled his arms back one at a time, and cuffed him. I heard approaching sirens and hurried back to the injured officer. He was sitting up now, his hand pressing against a wound on his shoulder. It was Cristo, the cop from Katlin's house. The one who had survived. He recognized me. "We have to stop meeting like this," he said with a faint smile on his face.

CHAPTER 36

POLICE FOUND THE abducted girl unconscious but alive in the car. They took the perpetrator into custody and subsequently identified him as responsible for at least two other kidnapping deaths near college campuses. Naturally, I had an exclusive on another high-profile case, but first I spoke to Rachel about what I should and shouldn't disclose, since the case would be in the court system for a while. Rachel advised I try to gloss over the details to avoid contaminating the jury pool or influencing jurors as the trial proceeded. My employer naturally opposed this, but I was cultivating a positive relationship with the police and the prosecutor's office—a rarity for an investigative journalist (most were ostracized by authorities for being bothersome or interfering with cases)—and I wanted to protect that. So, I followed her advice and let the wheels of justice roll slowly forward. In my interviews with Tilly and her team, I focused on the fear I'd felt during the abduction, for the victim, myself and Cristo. It satisfied them, and eventually I'd give them all the details they wanted.

I visited Cristo in the hospital. His eyes lit up when I walked in, but he was surrounded by his family—his mother, father, brothers, sisters, nieces, and nephews. His mother was a short Hispanic woman, full of energy and chattering excitedly in Spanish. She insisted I come over for dinner after Cristo was released from the hospital. After a while, Cristo asked his family if they could give him a few moments to talk with me alone. They went to the hospital cafeteria, and we enjoyed a pleasant conversation.

"Thank you for saving my life," he said. "I owe you one."

"You would have done the same for me, right?"

"Sure, but that's my job!"

"I thought you worked for Paradise Valley PD. Are you with Phoenix PD now?"

"Yeah, I applied to Phoenix PD, and they hired me. PPD is the big leagues, you know. If I'm going to be a cop, I might as well go big. Your cases in Paradise Valley were the most excitement in years over there. Here, we have two or three of those situations every weekend."

"You still want to be a cop after this?" I asked.

"Absolutely!" he said. "I'm just getting started."

Cristo asked me if I wanted to meet for coffee after his release. I said yes. My heart had been racing the entire time I was with him. I suppose I was nervous because I found him very attractive, and seeing him surrounded by his large family made me even more drawn to him. During high school, I spent a month every summer in Mexico on a church mission, helping to build homes for people who didn't have a place to live. I got to know many of the families we helped and was deeply moved by their love for each other. Those summer missions helped me augment my school-learned Spanish, and when I met Cristo's family, my fluency proved useful.

Cristo's mother and father emigrated legally from Mexico as young adults. His father worked for the power company as a *Zanjero*, a person responsible for maintaining the proper function of the canals. You may remember that I mentioned Phoenix metro has over 180 miles of canals, more than Amsterdam and Venice combined, so there was plenty of work for the Zanjero's. Cristo had three brothers, two sisters, and what seemed like dozens of nieces and nephews. They often gathered at his parents' house. I was surprised that such an attractive man as Cristo was neither married nor dating, but I had no complaints. We started seeing each other and our feelings for one another blossomed quickly.

Since he was new to the force, Cristo didn't have much seniority in the scheduling pool, so he often worked nights and weekends. In contrast, my schedule was completely flexible, allowing me to see him whenever he was free. I was also more than happy to have dinner at his parents' house on Sundays, which was much more than just dinner. It was an all-day affair. First, the family attended mass, then went out for breakfast after church. After that, the men played football in the backyard and watched the Cardinals on TV while the women cooked in the kitchen. Mrs. Perez was the head chef, but we all pitched in to assist her with the food preparation. There was always a large pot of pork green chili on the stove, along with posole, a Mexican hominy, and meat soup. The standout dish at the meal was often delicious tamales filled with chicken, pork, corn, cheese, and peppers.

The conversations in the Perez household were almost always in Spanish, and I was thankful for having learned the language earlier in my life. I felt the warmth of Cristo's wonderful family, and I knew he was under pressure from them to ask me to marry him from the very beginning. But he waited, and I wondered why. I didn't want to bring it up, but I thought it might be because his job was dangerous. He was acutely aware of everything I had lost in my life. I speculated he wanted to wait until he had advanced in seniority, at the very least, before proposing to me. If you're curious about what my answer would have been, it would've been yes. I loved Cristo from the start, and I was sure he loved me, too. But he never had the opportunity to ask.

CHAPTER 37

August 15, 2010
Sentencing Hearing

THE SHERIFF'S DEPUTY escorted me into the courtroom for my sentencing hearing. I was wearing the black-and-white uniform worn by inmates of MCSO (Maricopa County Sheriff's Office) at that time. I shuffled along, my ankles restricted by shackles connected by a chain, while my hands were in front of me, bound by handcuffs attached to a chain around my waist.

Looking out at the gallery, I saw my mother. She was sitting with Cristo's large family and was visibly sobbing. Cristo's mother was also crying, more emphatically than my mother. Cristo's father had his arm around Mrs. Perez and was looking at me tenderly. No one from the Perez family believed I had killed their son, and neither did the cops. A sea of blue filled the back of the gallery, featuring uniformed officers, in their dress blues, who had stood by me from the beginning. I was one of the few investigative reporters in the metro area who was a genuine friend of the police. Not only did I avoid interfering with their investigations, but I also twice helped bring murderers to justice, once saving the life of the man I'd been convicted of murdering. Almost all the police officers present that day had signed a written statement on my behalf, which was submitted to the judge for consideration during sentencing.

But the evidence against me was overwhelming. Cristo and I had an argument while out to dinner one evening. I was angry and was yelling at him, and it was quite a scene—very public, with many witnesses. I stormed out and took a taxi home alone. Later that night, someone murdered Cristo in his own home. I became a suspect because of the argument, and the police showed up at my home the next day with a warrant to search the premises. To my surprise, they found the murder weapon in my bedside drawer. It was the gun my mom had bought for me that had gone missing after the home invasion everyone thought was committed by Rick Miller. There were no prints on the gun except for mine.

Now I realize this set of facts is quite damning. So much so that a jury had convicted me. Perhaps even you are wondering if I actually did murder Cristo. That my heroic acts in recent years were simply one side of my story. You've seen that I tend to be high strung. That I have a temper. And you've seen that I've been willing to kill in the past, when I pulled the trigger while pointing a gun at Rick Miller, stopped only by a safety that I'd forgotten was still on. But I assure you, I am innocent. Again. And I intend to prove it to you.

I had avoided facing the death penalty for various reasons. Rachel explained some factors that the county attorney's office considers when making that determination—elements such as murder for hire, lying in wait, multiple victims, and the level of depravity in the killing itself. None of these factors were present in Cristo's murder. One shot to the center of the forehead at close range had killed him. It had been a closed-casket funeral, although I hadn't attended. This time, they jailed me from the beginning, even though Rachel argued for my conditional release pending trial. The judge had ruled against that, and since Cristo had been killed in November 2009, by the time of sentencing, I had already been in jail for ten months.

With the death penalty off the table, I was facing life in prison. The harshest option was life without parole, known as "natural life." The other possibility was life with the chance of parole. Unfortunately, even if I received the lighter sentence, state laws specified I wouldn't be eligible for parole until I had served twenty-five years. I was thirty-five, which meant I'd be sixty when I became eligible for parole. At that time, a parole board would hear my case for release and decide whether to grant or deny me parole. If denied, I'd have another chance a year later. This process would continue until my release or death. Reading these options, one might think that the judge's ruling hardly mattered. But that wasn't how I felt. Having the possibility of parole was at least something to give me hope. Otherwise, what reason did I have to live at all? Rachel had explained that an appeal was unlikely to be granted since the trial had transpired cleanly and without error. I really needed the judge to sentence me to life with the chance of parole.

They brought me to the counsel table, where Rachel stood and waited for me. The sheriff's deputy released the cuffs from the belly chain so I could sit. Rachel thanked him, but had one more request. "Sir, would you consider removing the cuffs?"

He didn't hesitate. "Of course, Ms. Cohen." He removed the cuffs.

Rachel looked at the bailiff. "We're ready," she said.

The bailiff notified the judge, and she entered the courtroom.

"All rise," said the bailiff. "The Honorable Maria Espinoza presiding."

"Please be seated," said the judge.

Everyone in the room sat down, and the proceedings began. The main purpose of this hearing was for the prosecution and defense to present facts that would help the judge impose a sentence appropriate for the crime I supposedly committed. I say supposedly, in case you don't remember me saying that I didn't do it. Unfortunately, the circumstantial evidence suggested otherwise. For me, today's proceeding was about whether or not I would receive hope. Would my future contain the faint possibility of regaining my freedom, or would my life end in prison?

What was most astonishing, not only to me but to virtually everyone involved in this case, including the prosecution, was that people didn't want to believe I had committed this crime. As I've mentioned before, my background and actions had been so law-abiding and supportive of the police and the justice system that it seemed beyond a reasonable doubt that I could even be here. Unfortunately, the jury had a duty to follow the law, and they did. After the verdict, when they were free to speak with the jurors, several of them told Rachel that their hearts told them I was innocent, but the circumstances presented a different story. That was nice to know, but it was cold comfort for someone now facing life in prison.

CHAPTER 38

April 2008

CRISTO, RUSTY, AND I arrived at the El Portal Inn in Sedona around 3 p.m. on a Tuesday. I had introduced Cristo to the El Portal a few months after we started dating. By April 2008, we had been together for over two years, and it had become one of our favorite spots since it was just two hours from Phoenix and incredibly welcoming to dogs. Cristo had fallen in love with Rusty from the beginning, just as I had. My mother was also smitten with the "Happy Drooler," as she affectionately called him, and it was always a challenge to pull him away from her. The two had grown quite attached, especially since my mom moved in with me. For this trip, I asked one of Mom's friends to hang out with her, and the two had a list of activities planned for the two days that Cristo, Rusty, and I would be in Sedona.

We settled in, and around six, the dog sitter

(recommended by the staff at El Portal) arrived, so Cristo and I went out for dinner. Rusty was on the sofa when we left, happily anticipating the snacks and walks that awaited him. Cristo and I dined at a reasonably priced restaurant called Creekside American Bistro. I would have preferred to splurge a bit more, and I had the money for it, but Cristo wouldn't hear of it. He was too proud to let me pay for anything, yet on a cop's salary, he couldn't make a habit of fine dining with a spoiled rich girl from Paradise Valley. The hotel bill alone would set him back substantially, but our midweek arrival helped keep the room rates more affordable.

Creekside offered a stunning view of the towering red rock formations that surrounded Sedona. I enjoyed a glass of wine while Cristo ordered a bottle of Dos Equis. After dinner, we returned to El Portal and settled with the sitter. We took Rusty for a walk down to the beautiful stream that flowed through the area, then made our way back to our room. I took a bottle of Sauvignon Blanc from the fridge and poured myself a glass. Cristo grabbed a beer, and we watched the news until we felt tired. Rusty had already fallen fast asleep on the sofa, so our lovemaking went unnoticed by the dog, which was typical. Our sounds of passion never seemed to disturb Rusty at all, as if it were just another part of life—a wonderfully exquisite part, as far as I was concerned.

The next morning, we walked Rusty, fed him, and enjoyed a continental breakfast in our room. Dressed in our hiking gear, we welcomed the dog sitter's arrival. After saying our goodbyes, we drove up Oak Creek Canyon to the West Fork Trailhead. The drive through the narrow, winding canyon was glorious, with peaks cloaked in conifer trees towering right next to the road. We paid the entrance fee for the park, parked the car, grabbed our daypacks and trekking poles, and set off down the trail. The path wound past old ruins and crossed back and forth over the bubbling Oak Creek at least six times during the four-mile hike. The poles came in handy while crossing the creek, allowing us to hop from rock to rock, though we still ended up getting wet. Fortunately, it was a beautiful spring day, with the sun shining brightly and the temperature around seventy-five degrees.

When the trail ended, we sat down and enjoyed a leisurely lunch. I'd made turkey sandwiches with avocado, tomato, lettuce, and cheese before we left Phoenix, and they were delicious. We washed it down with some unsweetened iced tea, munched on a few chips, and then headed back the way we came in. The towering red rock cliffs were magnificent and felt close enough to touch, and the colorful wildflowers dotting their sides were breathtaking. By the time we made it back to the car, we'd hiked over eight miles.

Back at the hotel, we paid the sitter, walked Rusty,

and then fed him. We stayed in that night, ordered takeout pizza from the nearby wood-fired pizzeria, and enjoyed a cozy dinner for two. Accompanied by Rusty, we went to the outdoor courtyard, which was surrounded by the various wings of the inn. A fire crackled in the fire pit as we roasted s'mores, also provided by the hotel. I had to wipe the drool from Rusty's mouth with a towel from our room, and I barely managed to keep him from stealing s'mores right off the stick from other hotel guests.

After another night of passionate lovemaking, we packed up the next morning and drove back to Phoenix. Short adventures like this became a way of life for Cristo and me, and I cherished them. My mistake was believing we would share experiences like this together for years to come. Unfortunately, the harsh realities of life took that from us.

CHAPTER 39

August 15, 2010
Sentencing Hearing
(continued)

IRST UP WAS the prosecutor, Sandra Jackson. She was the same lead prosecutor who had handled my trial. A seasoned homicide prosecutor, she was well-respected by the court, counsel, and law enforcement. We understood her stance from her sentencing memo, which outlined the pros and cons of leniency versus severity. It was significant that she hadn't made a convincing argument for life without parole, and I found some solace in that, believing it showed that the prosecutor's office also had doubts about the guilty verdict. Sandra gave her brief presentation and was back behind her table within five minutes.

Rachel was next. She outlined all the reasons

leniency would be appropriate and brought several members from the gallery into the well of the court to speak on my behalf. She called Cristo's father, Eduardo, to speak on behalf of the entire Perez family. Mr. Perez visited me several times at Estrella, before and after my conviction. I believe I mentioned he was a Zanjero, someone responsible for maintaining the canals that flow through the Valley. While this may seem like a mundane job to those not from the desert, it was vital to the well-being of the entire community and Zanjero's had the respect of all long-time Phoenix residents.

Mr. Perez had a confident bearing about him. His demeanor resembled what you'd expect from the best of cowboy culture. He was a man who had spent his entire life working outdoors, yet even when he wasn't on the job, he exuded a sense of dignity. In the courtroom, he always wore a collared shirt with a bolo tie and a brown suede jacket. He sported his dress Stetson when entering the courtroom, but removed it immediately after sitting down. When it was his turn to testify, he left the Stetson on the bench in the gallery and walked to the podium with measured steps, his head held high, but his eyes cast down. This was a difficult moment for him and my heart felt broken that he had to go through this. It had been his decision, however, and he wanted the world to know how he and his family felt about my role in Cristo's death.

Rachel introduced him. "Mr. Perez would like to speak on behalf of Ms. Moreland, your honor."

The judge leaned forward, obviously moved by the stately man's presence. "What would you like to tell me, Mr. Perez?" she asked. The judge's voice was kind and respectful. It was a touching moment to see such humanity from the person who would decide my fate.

Mr. Perez answered. "I speak on behalf of the entire Perez family. And for Cristo." He paused, trying to gather himself. "My son was a good man. He served the community bravely his whole adult life. We are so proud of him and look forward to the day when we are reunited with him. But the loss we feel is made worse by what has happened to Becky. We know in our hearts that she would never hurt Cristo. She would never hurt anyone. She saved my son's life! She helped many people. Our whole family loves her." Again, he paused. "It is painful to us that she will spend her life in prison for a crime she did not commit, and we beg you, judge, to show mercy on her. What you do here today affects all of us. Please, show mercy."

Mr. Perez walked slowly back to his seat in the gallery, a proud yet broken man. Each step of his cowboy boots echoed through the silent courtroom. I wiped the tears from my eyes and noticed others doing the same. Rachel took a deep breath and concluded her remarks. And then it was my turn. Rachel paved the way. "Your Honor, my client would like to address the court."

The judge nodded, and I stood, but my head was down. "I can barely speak right now, your honor, but I must. My heart is full of gratitude and love for my mother, the entire Perez family, and the many friends and law enforcement officers who are here today for Cristo and for me.

"It's hard for me to believe what's about to happen. I'm devastated." I raised my head now and looked Judge Espinoza right in the eye. "I didn't kill Cristo. I realize the verdict has been rendered. Nevertheless, I'm innocent. I ask you to show me mercy. To give me hope."

I sat down for a moment. Rachel reached over and touched me on the arm, squeezing gently. She was crying. I'd never seen her cry. The judge addressed Rachel. "Counsel, I'll give you a moment."

When Rachel had composed herself, she looked up at the judge and nodded. The judge spoke. "Ms. Moreland, please rise."

Rachel helped me to my feet, and we stood together.

"Rebecca Moreland, a jury has found you guilty of murder in the first degree. I presided at the trial, I have read and considered the pre-sentencing report and the sentencing memos provided by both counsel, and the statements made today in this courtroom. It is my duty to consider any aggravating and mitigating factors. I have found no aggravating factors. I have found several mitigating factors. Those are: your lack of criminal history, the evidence of your good work in the community, including your assistance in a murder investigation leading to the arrest of a multiple murderer, your intervention in an officer-involved shooting, where you subdued the assailant and rendered aid to an officer, and the overwhelming support we see in this courtroom today, from the Perez family, your mother, and members of law enforcement. This court has truly considered that the mitigating factors lead to the most merciful sentence I can impose, which is life with the possibility of parole in twenty-five years.

"It is hereby ordered that you be remanded to the custody of the Arizona Department of Corrections for the service of your sentence. You will receive credit for all pre-sentence incarceration. You have a right to appeal. There has been no claim for restitution; therefore, none will be ordered. Ms. Moreland, this court wishes you the best."

"All rise," said the bailiff.

The gallery rose. I was still standing, assisted by Rachel.

"We are adjourned," said the judge. She stood and left the courtroom.

There wasn't much clamor as the crowd filed out of the courtroom. I heard my mother and Mrs. Perez bawling, and others, too. Rachel led me to the bailiff's desk, where the bailiff asked me to put my thumbprint and signature on the sentencing paperwork.

The sheriff's deputy clipped my handcuffs to my belly chain and escorted me from the courtroom. Before I exited, I turned and smiled at my mother, giving her as much of a wave as I could, considering the bonds that restrained me.

CHAPTER 40

PERRYVILLE WAS A lonely place. It was the only women's prison in Arizona, housing over four thousand inmates. About thirty minutes west of Phoenix, they built it on barren desert land, creating a dusty environment that always required cleaning because of the blowing dust. The scent of cleaning chemicals lingered in the air, accompanied by the sound of metal doors opening and clanging shut. They classified me as a high-risk inmate because of my first-degree murder conviction. This resulted in highly restricted activities and movements during my first six months. I had a cell to myself, which had its advantages, but as time dragged on, I longed for human contact.

I was always friendly and cooperative with the guards, which eventually led to a reduction in my institutional risk classification. After that, I could work and participate in educational programs. However, most of the time, I was alone in my cell. I passed the time by practicing martial arts, which I had actively pursued for five years before my incarceration. I exercised as much as possible, even though the concrete floors provided little opportunity for effective workouts. More often than not, I daydreamed about my life before becoming a prisoner. One of my most vivid memories was the evening Cristo and I had argued; it was the last time I ever saw him.

We were out for dinner at one of our favorite restaurants, Chelsea's Kitchen, sitting outside. It was November, so there was a chill in the air. Many people don't realize that Phoenix is truly a desert environment: hot during the day and freezing at night. In the winter months, nightly temperatures can drop into the thirties. However, most restaurants offer outdoor seating year-round, placing tall portable heaters beside the tables in winter and using misters to provide cool, moist air during the summer.

Katlin Miller had joined us that evening, as she often did. I didn't understand why she had kept her last name. Rick was a notorious criminal, and his name was dirt in our town, especially among the police, since he had murdered one of their own. It would have made sense for Katlin to revert to her maiden name, but she didn't. To my knowledge, she hadn't even divorced Rick, but we never discussed it. Rick, now on death row and being held in the Rincon Unit in Tucson, was a person I never wanted to even think about. I assumed Katlin felt the same as I did about him: that he was a tragic, ugly memory best kept out of our daily lives. But I didn't really know how Katlin felt about Rick since we never talked about him. All I knew was that I forced myself to think of someone else if he ever crossed my mind. In November 2009, nearly five years had passed since they captured Rick and he stood trial for murdering four innocent people—Peter, my father, Rose Mendez, and Frank Hanson, the police officer at Katlin's home.

Since Rick's incarceration, Katlin had dated little. She claimed that the only men interested in her were older, wealthy guys, most of whom were married. She and I had become best friends, so we spent a lot of time together, usually at her house. I enjoyed being around her children, Ricky and Ashley, who were now nine and eight years old. Katlin didn't go out much, and Cristo and I felt sorry for her, so we sometimes invited her to join us. On the evening of the big argument between Cristo and me, Katlin was with us.

The dinner started well. Cristo was his normal, amiable self, encouraging Katlin to tell us about her kids. She said Ricky was a huge football fan and wanted to play. She planned on signing him up for a league next season. Ashley was a bookish little girl, always reading and fascinated with space. How an eight-year-old could read and enjoy science fiction was beyond me, but it was very impressive nonetheless.

After we finished the main course and ordered

dessert, Cristo excused himself to go to the restroom. He kissed me lightly on the lips before leaving the table. I distinctly remember how happy I felt at that moment. Cristo was the love of my life, and I was so proud of him. He had quickly risen through the ranks at PPD and was now studying for the exam to become a detective. I was ecstatic about this, not only out of pride in his accomplishments, but also because it would get him off patrol, which was terribly dangerous. A jolt of fear surged through me as I thought of the incident when the serial killer shot Cristo, and if not for my pepper spray, would have very likely killed him.

Katlin brought my reveries about Cristo to an abrupt halt. "Hey, Becky, there's something I need to tell you. Are you there?"

I shook myself back into the present. "Oh. Sure. Sorry about that."

"It's about Cristo," she said.

I raised my eyebrows. "What?" What could Katlin possibly tell me about Cristo that I didn't already know?

Katlin shuffled in her seat and scrunched her mouth up. She seemed uncomfortable. "I didn't want to say anything, but Cristo's been hitting on me."

I leaned back in my chair, my heart racing. I didn't know whether to be angry at Katlin or Cristo. Those who know me realize I'm high strung. My emotions can swing wildly, especially when faced with uncomfortable situations. I'll do anything necessary to resolve my issues, even resorting to physical force, as I had when I'd taken down Rick and the serial killer. In that moment, the urge to strike Katlin was boiling inside me, but then Cristo showed up at our table. He patted Katlin on the back and smiled at her, which enraged me so much that I lost control.

"Am I interrupting something?" I said, loudly enough for other diners to turn and look at our table.

"What?" he said. "What do you mean?"

"Are you having an affair with her?" I asked, too contemptuously.

Cristo looked wounded, but he was also hot-blooded. "What are you talking about, Becky?" His voice was also getting louder.

"I asked you a question?" I said, but I was so inside my head, so angry, that I didn't realize we'd disrupted the ambiance throughout the restaurant's outdoor dining area.

"We should go," he said, firmly. "This is no conversation to have here."

"I've got a better idea!" I yelled. "I'll leave, and you two lovebirds can go home together. I wouldn't want to intrude!"

I grabbed my purse and ran out of the restaurant. Cristo chased me, yelling at me to wait. When I got outside, I jumped into a taxi and told the driver to lock the doors because a man was pursuing me. He did as I asked, and we pulled quickly out of the lot. I gave the taxi driver my address, and he dropped me off there. I was still fuming, and my cell phone was burning up with calls from Cristo. I didn't answer them.

Fifteen minutes later, Cristo was pounding on my door. "Becky, please let me in," his voice said, muffled by the closed door but intelligible. Rusty was beside me, barking with anticipation because he knew Cristo's voice.

"Go away or I'm calling the police!" I yelled. "We'll see if you get a promotion after you're arrested for trespassing!"

After a moment, Cristo left. I went to the refrigerator and poured a glass of wine, pacing around, trying to calm down. My mother had gone out with friends, so it was just me and Rusty. I eventually settled down and tried to think about what had just happened. I'd gotten so furious that I hadn't even let Cristo talk to me. I called his cell phone several times, but he didn't answer. Then I heard a knock at my door. It was about an hour after Cristo had left my home. It was Katlin. I let her in.

We talked, and she described two encounters with Cristo that made her very uncomfortable. Honestly, as I recount this story, I can't even recall what they were. One thing I do remember is that Katlin's accusations against Cristo turned out to be blatant lies.

CHAPTER 41

MY FEELINGS FOR Katlin changed when a new prisoner arrived at Perryville. She was a Hispanic woman named Elena Garcia who had been convicted on a drug charge. She was serving ten years for possession with intent to sell. I met her in a self-improvement class called Conflict Resolution. I thought that since my inability to control my emotions had led to the argument with Cristo and other problems in my life, I should work on it. It was also an opportunity for socialization, although many of the inmates in this class were highly volatile. I had seen more than one fight break out right in the middle of the class.

Elena knew who I was, which wasn't unusual. Most people in Arizona recognized me. My first case, the murder of my husband, Peter Moreland, had made national headlines, especially when I reversed the situation by exposing Rick Miller and was ultimately found not guilty. The media highlighted my role in capturing Rick, especially after my employer's syndicated interview with me. Capturing the serial killer who drove the black panel van had put me on top of the news world. After that, my career in investigative journalism skyrocketed. My articles were syndicated nationwide and read widely. But then, everything came to an abrupt halt.

My conviction for murdering Cristo plunged me into the abyss of public opinion. I was labeled a cop killer, and society despises cop killers. On the flip side, being a known murderess came with certain advantages inside prison. Inmates often thought twice before confronting a cold-blooded killer. At least some of them did. Elena was one of those. She kept her distance from me, but whenever I glanced in her direction, she flashed a mischievous smile, as if she knew something but wouldn't share it. One day, I decided to find out what it was.

My first extended encounter with Elena Garcia happened outside in the prison yard. I was sitting on a bench in the yard, minding my own business, during my one-hour daily outdoor period, when I noticed Elena milling about. She was alone at the moment. I stood up and approached her, stepping in front of her to block her path. She looked up, recognized me, and smiled. "Hello, Ms. Moreland," she said respectfully.

"Hi, Elena. I don't mind if you call me Becky."

"Okay," she said. "What can I do for you?"

"I'd like to talk for a minute if you don't mind."

"About what?"

I shrugged my head toward the bench I'd been sitting on. It was still empty. "Why don't we sit down and chat."

She nodded, and we went to the bench and sat. I noticed she kept as far away from me as possible, suggesting she was afraid of me. "What do you want to talk about, Becky?" she asked.

"You seem to know me, Elena. Do you?"

"Everyone knows who you are," she said.

"But you know more than most, don't you?" I asked.

"I saw you a few times, in Paradise Valley. At the Miller residence."

"Katlin Miller's?"

"Yes, I worked for Juanita's Maid Service for a long time. Until I got in trouble."

"So you cleaned the Miller's home for them?"

"Yes, for many years. I started when Mr. Rick still lived there. But then, he went away and it was only Mrs. Miller, and the children."

"I see." I sensed that Elena had more to tell me. Was it about Katlin? "Was Mrs. Miller a good employer?"

"At first, yes. But then she changed."

"How did she change, Elena?'

"She always used to be nice. Very friendly. But as the years went by, she seemed to become more angry. She yelled at us a lot. And then, one day, I saw her somewhere."

This was becoming interesting. "Saw her where? What was she doing, Elena?"

"She was near where I live, on the south side of town. I saw her coming out of a gun range there. A lot of criminals use that range because it's inside, and they don't ask for I.D. or gun registration."

Hmmmm. "What do you think she was doing there?"

"At first, I didn't know. But then, when I was cleaning her house, I saw a gun in her bedroom. It was sitting on the desk in there. I thought then that maybe she was practicing shooting at the gun range."

I didn't even know Katlin owned a gun. And if she did, why would she drive all the way to the south side to practice? There were plenty of gun ranges on the east side of Phoenix, near where she lived. It didn't make sense. But since I had Elena there with me, I thought I'd try to find out more.

"Did you see anything else in her home that you found odd?

"That day when I saw the gun, beside it was a gun silencer."

"Was it attached to the gun?"

"No, it wasn't. Maybe she took it off so she could carry them in her purse. I don't know."

Was this even possible? The evidence at Cristo's home, which was in a modest neighborhood near the 51 freeway, might help me put something together with the new information Elena was conveying. They found him collapsed on the threshold of his open front door, a 9-millimeter bullet lodged in the back of his skull after tearing his brain to shreds. Police had interviewed all the neighbors. No one had heard or seen anything. No one in the neighborhood had cameras on their homes, and Ring Video Doorbells didn't exist in 2009. The point was that no one heard a gunshot. Someone would have had to shoot Cristo with a silenced gun. During my trial, Rachel contended that neither my mother nor I possessed a silencer, but the fact persisted: forensic analysis had already identified the gun in my home as the murder weapon because small amounts of Cristo's blood and cranial matter were found on it. Case closed. Until now.

"Why do you think she became angry over the years, Elena?'

"I don't know," she said. "But maybe it had something to do with Mr. Rick being in prison."

"What causes you to think that?"

"One day, I heard her talking on the phone with him. I don't know what he said, but it made her very angry."

"Did she say something to him that made her seem angry?"

"Yes, she said something like: 'Why should I care if Becky got all the money? It's your fault, anyway!"

Oh my, oh my. Where was this leading?

CHAPTER 42

ACCESSED ONE OF the prison phones reserved for privileged conversations and called Rachel, telling her I urgently needed to meet with her. She arrived the next day, and we met privately in a visitation room designated for privileged meetings. I recounted everything I had learned from Elena. At first, Rachel was silent. I was eager to hear her thoughts, but I had learned through years of working with her that Rachel approached her work methodically. Patience was crucial, though waiting wasn't easy for me. It never had been, and I was serving a life sentence as a result.

Eventually, she spoke. "We should preserve Elena's testimony as soon as possible because there are people who wouldn't want her to testify in court if it ever gets that far."

"Like Katlin? She's not involved with the criminal underworld. She couldn't arrange a killing on the inside."

"Probably not," said Rachel. "But she was allegedly seen at a shady gun shop in South Phoenix. That place is a haven for people in the criminal underworld. And then there's Rick. He's been in prison for over five years. Who knows what contacts he's made along the way?"

"Okay, just let me know when you want to do it. I think I can get her to cooperate."

Rachel nodded.

"What else?" I asked.

"We need to verify that Elena Garcia is who she says she is. Did she really work for Juanita's Maid Service? Did she clean the Miller's home for all the years she said she did? What is she really in prison for? Was it truly drugs, or something with a lighter sentence?"

"You mean she could be a plant?"

"Not likely. There's nothing to gain by setting you up again, Becky. You're doing life already. We just need to provide as much credibility to the witness as possible. After all, she's a convicted felon. Her testimony will be diluted by that alone."

"What else can we do to make this stick?"

"Make it stick on who? Katlin?"

"Yeah, and maybe Rick, too. Maybe they're in it together."

Rachel paused, thinking. "I'll have my investigator visit the gun shop to find out what he can. A beautiful blonde from Paradise Valley would be radically out of place there and would be remembered by anyone who saw her. I don't expect the guy to tell us much because he probably has a lot to hide and a reputation to keep with the criminals who use his range, but it might be something."

"Anything else?"

"My investigator might have some ideas. I'll get back to you as soon as we have something more to discuss."

Rachel came back to see me about a week later. Her investigator met with the gun range's owner, who remembered Katlin. He said she came in there a few times a week for about a month in the fall of 2009, but he couldn't remember the exact dates.

"Cristo was murdered in the fall of 2009," I said. "So that's consistent."

"It is," said Rachel. "But there's something else even more interesting. The guy remembered that she used a Smith & Wesson handgun."

"That's what my gun was!" I said.

"Yes, but there are a lot of Smith & Wesson handguns in the world, Becky. That alone doesn't count for much. But there's something else that gives us a sliver of hope."

"What?"

"The gun shop owner told my investigator that Katlin always practiced with a silencer. You remember when I argued that a silencer would have had to be used in the murder because no shots were heard by neighbors? And since you didn't own or have access to a silencer, you couldn't have committed the murder?"

"Yeah, but we always knew that was a weak argument."

"It was, but now it can help point a finger at Katlin, especially if we can track down the silencer. Frankly, it doesn't seem likely we'll find it, but she's already made one mistake."

"What?"

"She bought the silencer from the shady gun shop where she practiced. And she paid for it with a credit card."

I was getting excited. "This is great news! Is there anything else?"

"Yes, there is. My investigator thought it might be good to visit Rincon, where Rick is being held on death row."

"And?"

"Katlin visited Rick dozens of times in the years before Cristo's murder, and has been there six times since you were convicted."

"That's weird, but is it relevant?"

"We don't know, but most visitations there are recorded, just like at Estrella and Perryville. We can access those tapes if we can get the prosecutor to cooperate. The same applies to any phone calls between them."

"Do you think we can get the prosecutor on board?" I asked.

"I do. And I also think that as soon as we get the statement from Elena Garcia, we'll have enough to seek a warrant to search Katlin's home and car."

CHAPTER 43

ELENA GARCIA AGREED to give her statement to Rachel. She seemed to enjoy spending time with me, and I had no issue with her company. She appeared to be a decent young woman who had gotten involved with the wrong crowd. I couldn't promise her anything, nor could Rachel, but I hoped that her role in assisting my case might eventually be a feather in her cap with the authorities. I figured that would depend on whether or not we succeeded.

The recordings of all of Katlin's meetings with Rick didn't reveal a detailed plan between the two of them to frame me for Cristo's murder. However, there was a significant amount of discussion about me, mostly portraying me as a con artist who'd robbed Rick and Katlin of their hard-earned wealth. I was taken aback by Katlin's hostility toward me; I never sensed that when we were together. But it was hard to overlook. "I hate her!" she exclaimed to Rick in one recording. "She's rich and in love, while I have nothing! She stole my husband and my money!" Statements like that, and others, established a motive.

Rachel's investigator got the receipt for Katlin's silencer purchase from the gun shop owner. Rachel took this receipt, along with the investigator's other findings and Elena Garcia's testimony, to the prosecutor assigned to my case, Sandra Jackson. Rachel argued that all this newly discovered evidence pointed to Katlin Miller as the true murderer of Cristo Perez. Sandra presented the issue to her supervisors, who instructed her to notify the police about the Katlin Miller case. The police then sought a warrant to search Katlin Miller's home and car. During the search, police found the silencer in Katlin's car's glove compartment, and they immediately arrested her. I wondered if the kids were there and worried about them, but Rachel told me that Child Protective Services accompanied the police, and they had taken the kids to Katlin's parents. Rachel had been told they were doing okay. I was glad things were moving in the right direction for me, but I felt a mix of emotions, from anger toward Katlin to pure empathy for her kids.

Here's the conclusion everyone reached regarding Katlin's actions on the night of the murder. After I stormed out of the restaurant, she drove to Critso's house and waited for him. You will remember that Cristo immediately came to my home, but I had rebuffed him. Trust me, the guilt I feel because I didn't invite him in has never left me. Not only did I fail to give him a chance to refute Katlin's accusation, I very likely caused his death by not letting him in and apologizing for my outburst. But I let him leave, and when he arrived home, Katlin greeted him. Because he was polite, he opened his door and was about to let her into the house. But when he turned around to see if she was following him in, she already had the gun out and pointed at him. She pulled the trigger and shot him in the forehead. She then drove to my home, supposedly to console me, but took the extended time we had spent together to excuse herself to use the restroom and stealthily planted the gun in my bedside table drawer. Katlin was admitting to none of this, but it all made sense. She would stand trial for her actions.

Rachel also informed me that the prosecutor's office had agreed to a post-conviction hearing to reopen my case. Just so you know, a post-conviction hearing determines whether a defendant like me has presented enough new evidence to warrant another trial. This was what happened the first time around when Rick framed me for Peter's murder, and it happened again this time. The judge granted post-conviction relief, and Sanda Jackson, the prosecutor, stood up and told the court that the state would not pursue a case against me and moved to dismiss my case. The judge granted this, and I was free. My mom picked me up outside the prison gate and drove me home. Needless to say,

I felt tremendous relief, but it would be a lie to say I was happy. I'd lost too many loved ones to feel that way. Perhaps one day, I'd find a cure for my anguish, but I saw no path for that happening for a long time.

CHAPTER 44

April 22, 2011
Katlin Miller's Plea-
Change Hearing

T HE PROSECUTION SOUGHT the death penalty
in Katlin's case. There were just too many
aggravating factors. She'd been planning the
killing for months, with every action she took that
night carefully orchestrated to frame me. She'd practiced shooting to ensure she got it right when the time
for killing Cristo arrived. And she'd been lying in wait
for him just before the killing. Undoubtedly, this was a
death penalty case, and the judge agreed. Katlin would
stand trial for her life for the murder of Cristo Perez,
the love of my life. Unless. Unless her defense team
could work out a plea deal with the prosecution.

Let me explain. At Katlin's arraignment, the court
entered a not-guilty plea on her behalf. However, as

time passed, and she contemplated facing the death penalty, she must have asked her attorneys whether it was possible to negotiate a deal for life without parole instead of death. Apparently, she provided enough information to persuade the prosecution to agree. However, the agreement needed to be ratified by a judge, which required Katlin to admit in open court what she had done and how.

I wanted very badly to be there, and since I'd been released by that time, I could attend. Some might wonder why, since I would have to relive the death of the person I had loved more than any other in my life. But my answer to you is simple. I wanted to hear her say that she did it. So did the entire Perez family, my mom, and all the cops and family friends who knew Cristo. All of us were there that day. The press was also there in force. It was national news. Again. I'd once again been vindicated and here was the person who did it this time around.

A sheriff's deputy helped Katlin to the podium after she was sworn in; she shuffled slowly because of the shackles on her ankles and her cuffed hands. I noticed she had some papers in her hand, and assumed this was her statement. No doubt her attorneys had helped draft it so that it complied with the requirements of the plea hearing. She awkwardly placed the papers on the lectern and looked at the judge.

The judge addressed her. "Mrs. Miller, I have your

plea agreement in front of me. You've agreed to plead guilty to murder in the first degree. In order for me to accept your plea, you must now provide a factual basis for what you did and how you did it. Are you ready to proceed?"

Katlin nodded, and the judge admonished her. "You must say 'yes' or 'no,' Mrs. Miller, so the court reporter can type your answer into the record. So, I ask you, Mrs. Miller, are you ready to make your statement?"

"Yes," Katlin replied. I couldn't determine what she was feeling at that moment, but she appeared pale, and her brow was glistening with sweat. She looked as if she had caught the flu and might vomit at any second.

"Please proceed," said the judge.

Katlin took a deep breath and looked down at her notes. "I killed Cristo Perez. I had planned to do this for months. My desire to do this came from animosity toward Rebecca Moreland, which had built up over the years. I saw my life in shambles while hers blossomed. I blamed her for all my pain. If I could kill the person I knew she loved and set things up to appear as if she had done it, I thought I would find peace.

"My husband had stolen Becky's gun during a home invasion and given it to me. He told me never to handle the gun without wearing gloves since it still had Becky's fingerprints on it. I kept it hidden and didn't tell anyone, including the police. I devised a plan to make Becky angry with Cristo in a public place where there would be witnesses. As the time approached for me to complete my plan, I bought a gun silencer and started practicing shooting at a gun range, always wearing thin gloves to keep my prints off the gun. As soon as I was confident I could fire the weapon properly and accurately, I knew I was ready.

"Becky, Cristo, and I often dined out together. On the evening of the murder, we ate at Chelsea's Kitchen. I remember rehearsing what I had planned when I drove myself over to meet them at the restaurant. When Cristo left the table to go to the restroom, I told Becky that Cristo had been making advances toward me. I knew she would believe me because I am an attractive woman, and Becky has seen many men looking at me with desire over the years. Becky reacted the way I had hoped she would. I knew she had a quick temper and struggled to control her emotions. She is an impulsive person.

"As soon as Becky left the restaurant, Cristo ran after her. I knew he would follow her, and my hope was that she would reject him and that he would eventually go home. After the two of them were gone, I drove to Cristo's neighborhood, parked my car on another street, and walked to his house under the cover of darkness. I waited near his front door for about thirty minutes, and he arrived. He didn't have a garage, so he pulled into his tiny driveway and approached me.

"I told him I was there to make sure he was okay. He was in no mood to see me, but being the gentleman he was, he turned to the front door to unlock it, intending to let me in. While he was turned away from me, I withdrew the gun from under my coat, raised it, and pointed it at his head. I was wearing the thin pair of gloves that I always wore when handling the gun. When he turned to me to make sure I was following him in, I fired the gun once. The bullet hit him in the center of his forehead. He fell and lay there on the threshold of the door.

"I left him there and hurried away from the house into the dark. There were no streetlights on his street, and I hoped this would enable me to escape with no one seeing me. I drove immediately to Becky's home. I removed the silencer from the gun to make room for the gun in my purse. I threw the silencer in the glove compartment, closed the purse and went to Becky's front door. When she answered, I said I was there to make sure she was okay. She wasn't, but seemed like she wanted company. She was agitated because she'd been calling Cristo and he hadn't answered. She was thinking of driving to his home, but I talked her out of it. I told her she should give it twenty-four hours to allow for both of them to calm down. What she didn't know was that Cristo was already dead, and that is why he wasn't answering the phone.

"During my time at Becky's, I asked her if I could

use the restroom. She went to the kitchen to pour more wine, and I went straight to her bedroom and placed the gun in her bedside table drawer, which is where it had been when Rick stole it. I used a handkerchief so I wouldn't leave fingerprints on the gun. I was back in my seat in the den before she even returned with the wine.

"The next day, the police searched Becky's home and found the gun. She was arrested. I was a witness at her trial, testifying that I'd witnessed the argument. I admitted that I had told Becky of Cristo's advances toward me, and I testified that it was true that he had done this. But it was a lie. I also lied about where I'd gone after the incident at the restaurant. I claimed that I had gone home, but since I was worried about Becky, I decided to go see her about an hour after I'd gone home. I've already stated what really happened. I'd gone directly to Cristo's and waited for him, then went to Becky's after I killed him.

Katlin paused, then drew in another deep breath. "I knew what I was doing, and I knew that it was wrong. If I had it to do over again, none of this would have ever happened."

And that was her statement.

"Are there any additions or corrections to the factual basis?" asked the judge.

"No, your honor," said the prosecutor.

"I find that sufficient evidence has been presented.

I am accepting the plea. It's ordered that this matter be set for sentencing on June 13. This court is adjourned."

The sheriff's deputy led Katlin out of the courtroom. My mom hugged me, and we all left the gallery. I received so many warm embraces from Cristo's family that I was sore the next day. I must admit, it felt wonderful for Katlin to confess everything for the world to see, but at the same time, I felt an undercurrent of sadness. As the days passed, the sadness didn't fade. I wondered if it was grief over the loss of Cristo. That was undoubtedly there, but something else tugged at my heart, too. Then I figured it out. I felt sorry for Katlin. Although she was a deeply troubled individual, Katlin was also a mother of two innocent children; their grandparents would raise them because both parents were in prison. I wanted to help those kids, so I arranged to visit Katlin at Perryville.

CHAPTER 45

VISITING KATLIN WASN'T as simple as making an appointment. Her sentence prohibited her from having any contact with victims. Katlin was guilty not only of murdering Cristo but also of conspiring to frame me. Hence, I was one of her victims. For me to see her, assuming, of course, that she agreed to see me, we had to get an order from the judge carving out an exception to the general prohibition against contact with victims, except for me. Rachel worked with the prosecutor and Katlin's attorney to make a motion for this, and the judge granted it. Anyway, I could meet with her, and was happy she'd agreed to it. This was a good six months after she'd been sentenced, and we met at my old stomping grounds, Perryville.

My heart started pounding when I passed by the old brown sign, shaped like the state of Arizona, that read "ARIZONA STATE PRISON COMPLEX, PERRYVILLE." There was a time not so long ago when I'd believed I'd spend my whole life there. Then I met Elena Garcia, and things had changed. Now, it was Katlin Miller who would spend her life inside Perryville.

Katlin and I met in the general visitation area. Several other inmates in the room had visitors, too. Katlin was in ankle cuffs, a belly chain, and handcuffs for the visit. We sat opposite one another at a table that resembled a picnic table. But it was no picnic for her or for me.

I opened up with a question I'd had since the visit had come together. "I was wondering why you agreed to see me."

"That's easy," she said. "I don't get many visitors. I'm lonely."

"And you'd even accept me, the person you hate most, just to have someone to talk to?"

"Yeah," she said. "Why not? I realize now how warped my thinking was, Becky. I don't hate you. I hated myself for allowing myself to become completely dependent on Rick. I couldn't take care of myself, even though you made sure I had money to help me do it."

I wondered if Katlin truly meant what she was saying or was simply repeating words she'd heard from a counselor at the prison. After all, she'd only been in prison for six months. From what Rachel told me, when inmates genuinely came to terms with what they had done, it typically happened over many years. Still, I went along with it, giving her the benefit of the doubt. "That's good to hear. So you've been taking advantage of some classes here? Is that how you're starting to figure things out?"

"Absolutely," she said.

"I'm glad your plea deal went through," I said.

"Thank you," she said. "Luckily, Rick had given me the account information for where he'd hidden his money offshore. I turned that over as part of my plea deal."

I had wondered if she had sweetened the pot to get the death penalty reduced to life without parole. "Do you mind if I ask how much he'd stashed there?"

"A few million dollars," she said. "But there was no easy way to get the money back into the country. I would have had to travel to Belize and smuggle it back in as cash, bit by bit. I wasn't going to do that."

"So he went to Belize when he escaped the first time, huh?"

"Eventually. Belize has no extradition with the United States."

I didn't know what to say next, but Katlin helped me focus. "Why are you here, Becky? Do you plan to write this as one of your news stories?"

"I haven't gone back to work," I said. "I'm not sure if I'll ever go back."

"Hmmm," she mused. "So what is it, then? I mean, how could you possibly want to see me?"

And then it just came out. "I wanted you to know that I can help with the kids, if you want me to."

Katlin's reaction to my offer was sudden. Her face contorted and she broke down in tears. She sobbed for a long time, and I wondered what she was thinking. She tried to wipe her tears away, but her cuffs made it hard. I reached for a tissue and started to hand it to her, but then I remembered the rules—no contact—so I pulled the tissue back and held it in my hand as I waited for Katlin to gain control of her emotions. Eventually, she had recovered enough to speak, sniffling between words. "I don't know, Becky," she sputtered. "That's a lot to take in. It confuses me."

"I understand. I didn't believe it either when I started thinking about it."

Listen, folks. I realize that some of you might wonder if I truly meant what I said to Katlin, about wanting to help with her kids. Others may even question my sanity. You all know what she did to Cristo. And to me. But have you considered what I did? I lost my temper at the mere mention of Cristo's infidelity. I didn't even give him a chance to talk to me about it, to tell me it wasn't true. Katlin herself testified during the hearing, to save her own life, that it hadn't happened. This was a hearing where it was crucial for her to speak the truth or face the death penalty. He'd done nothing wrong, and I didn't grant him the benefit of the doubt. Because of that, he went home to his death. I hope this helps you understand the guilt I was carrying. I believed my offer to help Katlin's kids was sincere, and here's why: it was part of my own journey toward absolution. If I could forgive Katlin, perhaps I could forgive myself.

Katlin composed herself. "Do you really mean it?" she asked.

"I do, Katlin. I forgive you for what you did. And by helping you, trust me when I tell you that I'll be helping myself. Your kids need as much love and support as they can get, and so do I."

I could see that Katlin was on the brink of breaking down again, but she got out a few more words. "Thank you, Becky. My kids need someone good in their lives right now."

"Is that a yes?"

Katlin took a deep breath. "I think it is. I'm struggling to believe you would do this for me, but I also understand what you're saying about forgiveness. Forgiving myself is something I'll be working on for the rest of my life, but I really hope I succeed because the pain is unbearable. The guilt is crushing."

"You can do it, Katlin. We can do it."

And then, my first meeting with my recently convicted and former best friend ended. We'd each carry on with sorrow in our hearts, trying to be better human beings than we'd been before.

Epilogue

January, 2013

I BELIEVE THE SAYING "Time heals all wounds" is mostly accurate, although it doesn't truly address the nature of healing. Inevitably, some wounds leave deep scars. Katlin and I were scarred in ways neither of us would ever fully comprehend. But now, we were both trying to smooth out those scars. She was in prison, while I was on the outside, but when we agreed I would help her children, we found a salve that might just aid in the healing.

I started visiting the children regularly. They were living with Katlin's parents, who had helped them change their last names to Katlin's maiden name, Pendergast. Ricky and Ashley Pendergast. The Pendergasts moved to another part of town, and I offered to pay for the kids to attend a private school. Few, if any, of the children at their new school knew who their birth parents were, and they had made a decent start in their new lives, receiving plenty of counseling and learning how to cope with the realization that both of their parents were in prison for life. Rick would eventually be executed, and Katlin would be in Perryville until the day they carried her out in a body bag.

On a clear Phoenix day in early January, Eduardo and Sofia Perez, parents of the deceased Cristo Perez, hosted a gathering at their home. It was no different from most Sundays. Church in the morning, breakfast out after that, then cooking in the kitchen and football outside in the backyard. On this day, I was outside watching the boys and men play football. I had Ricky and Ashley with me. Now eleven, Ashley felt comfortable enough to go inside with one of Cristo's nieces to help prepare the big afternoon meal. My mom was in the kitchen, too, throwing in her two cents about how to cook tamales, probably. Ricky, twelve, was playing football. I stood watching, standing beside my old friend, Rachel Cohen, and her husband, Phil. Their son, Adam, was taking part in the football game. Rusty ran around in the fenced-in backyard, fetching balls and playing with whoever was interested in him. He was still reasonably spry at twelve years old.

It had been three years and two months since Cristo died, and I hadn't dated during that time. I hadn't worked either. After I was found innocent again, Tilly called to see if I wanted to return to work. I wasn't inclined to accept, but I gave her another exclusive, for which she was very grateful. Tilly mentioned the door was always open for me, and we kept in touch. I spent more and more time with Ricky and Ashley, who had taken to calling me "Aunt Becky." I visited Katlin whenever I could manage it, but every time I drove up to Perryville and saw that brown sign shaped like the state of Arizona, my heart fluttered. It was a place that was really hard to return to.

As I watched the football game, I felt a sense of belonging unlike any I'd ever known, which always happened when I visited with the Perez family. This was a place I would always come back to when I needed to ground myself. Just then, Eduardo, Cristo's dad, approached me and stood beside me. He put his arm around me as he would with one of his own daughters, and it comforted me to know that's exactly how he thought of me.

"How you doin', Mija?" he asked. Mija was a term of endearment used by Mexican fathers with their daughters. Eduardo liked to call me that. I liked it too, and I had my own term of endearment for him.

"I'm doing great, Papa."

"What's going on in your life?" he asked. "Have you gone back to work?"

"Not yet, but I've been keeping busy with Ricky and Ashley."

"They're good kids," he said. "It's good of you to help them."

"Thank you, Papa."

"What about a man in your life?" he asked, surprising me. "It's time for you to consider that possibility, don't you think?" His question shook me; I struggled to answer, and he noticed this, continuing to speak. "Life is meant to be lived, Becky. All the Perez family would welcome any man you love into our family. I want you to know that."

I remained quiet, and my mind inevitably slipped to Cristo. I remembered the love we had shared, and scenes from the many beautiful experiences we'd had together flashed through my mind. I tried to fight off the tears, but they came anyway. I felt the rough fingers of Papa's hands brushing away my tears. "Enough tears, Mija. Enough tears."

"I miss him so much," I whispered.

"Me too," he said. "But life goes on, my lovely daughter. You've received a gift from God, giving you a second chance at life. Please, live the time you have left here to the fullest. Open your heart to what comes your way. Be at peace with the things you cannot change. Can you do that for me, Mija?"

Papa's words calmed my heart and soul. I was able to hear them. To understand them. And from that moment forward, I believed in them. "Yes, Papa. I can do that for you. And for Cristo."

"He is in heaven waiting for you. But he wants you to be happy here on Earth."

"I am happy, Papa. But I agree. I can do more to live life to the fullest. And I will."

THE END

Turn the page to read Chapter 1 of *One More Life to Live,* another standalone novel in the *Second Chance Novel series.*

CHAPTER 1

St. Augustine's School, London/1948

THE RULER SLAMMED down on Edward's knuckles, the crack of its impact echoing off the ceiling and walls of the sparsely furnished classroom.

"That should teach you!" came the high-pitched voice of Sister Evelyn, a stout woman in her mid-fifties. Spittle from her mouth scattered onto his face, her acrid breath washing over him.

Edward, a tall, thin boy of ten, was distinctly aware of the pain in his fingers and intensely nauseated by the nun's stinking exhalation. But he didn't flinch. Nor did he squeal. His expression was serene. His answer was the same sound that had gotten him in trouble to begin with—a loud release of intestinal gas issuing from his bottom. Edward's classmates erupted in laughter.

"Silence!" screamed the nun, and the class fell mute. "You want another then, do you?"

She raised her makeshift club and prepared for another strike, having already inflicted five sharp blows, typically more than enough to force a child to relent. But Edward Stubbins believed his insolence was fully justified, not only by the fate he'd endured thus far in his young life but also from sheer hatred of the institution where he'd been imprisoned.

"Wail away, sister," said Edward with calm confidence. "Beating children is, after all, one of your few great joys in life."

Sister Evelyn hesitated, her eyebrows raising, seemingly at a loss for words. The other boys in the classroom sat wide-eyed and absolutely silent, waiting for the ruler to fall one more time, perhaps breaking Edward's bleeding and swelling fingers.

The wooden bludgeon remained poised and still in the air. The nun was momentarily paralyzed, but Edward could see from her eyes that her mind was whirling. What was she thinking? Had his words hit home? They must have.

"Class dismissed," said Sister Evelyn. "Go to your rooms and study until the noon meal."

The boys rose in unison and scurried toward the door.

Edward attempted to follow but was deterred by

the nun's firm grip on his wrist. "Not you, Master Stubbins. You and I must speak."

Edward fell back into his chair and waited for his punishment to continue. The last boys exited, leaving him and Sister Evelyn alone in the cavernous room. The orphanage had been hastily set up after the war in a warehouse that had been used to store munitions. The rooms were all large and cold and uninviting, haphazardly renovated to house the children displaced by the loss of their parents during the relentless German bombings of London.

Edwards's father had been killed during the D-Day assault on the shores of France. His mother had died when their apartment complex was hit by a bomb. Edward was out playing in the street during the bombing and was spared any harm, notwithstanding the damage to his psyche from the war and the loss of his parents. He'd been seven years old.

Edward had lived on the streets for nearly a month, begging for food and sleeping in cemeteries, parks, and vestibules of bombed-out buildings, but he was ultimately scooped up by volunteers patrolling the streets for displaced children like himself. He was taken to St. Augustine's School, where he'd lived for the past three years.

When people visited the school, looking for children to adopt, Edward and his mates were herded en masse for viewings. Inevitably, however, one of

Edward's fellow residents was selected. The nuns told him he needed to smile more, look people in the eye, and eat more food so that he could fill out a bit. They claimed he looked unhealthy, as if he were diseased and frail, and that no one would ever take a child home that looked like that. His thin blond hair gave the appearance of balding, further exacerbating his pathetic appearance. Hence, he was never chosen. And it seemed to Edward that his undesirability caused him to be viewed by the nuns as a liability. A nuisance to be tolerated but not cultivated.

When Edward acted out in class, as he had that morning, entertaining his mates with his trumpeting and odiferous emissions, the hateful nuns enthusiastically punished him. Edward's view was that the gas was directly attributable to the certifiably rotten cuisine provided at St. Augustine's, and he was rarely inclined to hold it in. Why should he suffer the indignity of a swollen and painful belly? It was but a small sacrifice to take a beating for demonstrating what living at St. Augustine's had done to him.

"Edward, Edward, Edward," said Sister Evelyn, now seated behind her desk in the front of the room. "What shall we do with you?"

Edward pulled a handkerchief from his pockets and dabbed it on his bleeding knuckles. "Let me leave, perhaps," he suggested.

"And where would you go? What would you eat?

What shelter would you find? No, Edward, you may not leave. The world is a cruel place, lad. You'll learn that soon enough."

Edward lifted his gaze from his bleeding hand. "But sister, haven't I already discovered that?"

Once again, Sister Evelyn seemed at a loss for words. She bowed her large head, and the dark veil of her habit draped down over her broad shoulders. Clasping her hands together, she prayed.

"Lord, give me the strength to help this boy. Please show me the path that would best serve you. In the name of the Father, the Son, and the Holy Spirit, I pray."

The nun remained hunched over in the position of prayer as if she were waiting for instructions from God to come to her. Edward, while only ten, was distinctly aware of his exceptionally well-developed intellect, and he had no intention of accepting God into his life. On the contrary, he scoffed at the fuss the priests, nuns, and their parishioners made over this wholly invisible, allegedly all-powerful being. Nevertheless, he was at the mercy of these people and totally dependent on them for his survival. Despite his awareness of his precarious position, he couldn't bring himself to submit to their foolish rules and customs.

"Any word from above?" he chided.

Sister Evelyn's head rose slowly, and her expression seemed to have changed from one of deference to her lord to that of a fire-breathing dragon about to vaporize a helpless group of onlookers. Her eyes were wide and menacing, and her mouth curled into a hideous scowl.

"Yes, Master Stubbins. I have received God's message. You will be sent to Australia along with the next shipment of orphans heading in that direction. I'm sure you will fare much better there than you have here."

Continue reading *One More Life to Live* from *the Second Chance Novel series:*

Amazon link: https://mybook.to/0pxCI
or go to
www.stevendecker.com

Acknowledgments

My heartfelt thank you to my wife, Karen, who reads every word I write, and who has a more expansive vocabulary than dictionary.com. Her insights into character development, plot lines, and narrative are profoundly helpful to me. But it's safe to say I wouldn't have been able to write *Innocent Again* at all without Karen by my side. Her expertise as a trial attorney was not only invaluable, it was essential. Thank you, my love, for being you.

About the Author

Steven Decker lives and writes in both Arizona and Connecticut and travels throughout the world looking for new ideas and settings for his books. He enjoys spending time with Karen and Mr. Wilson, the beagle, walking in the countryside, and spending precious time with his children and their families.

Visit www.stevendecker.com to learn more about the author and the wide range of novels he has written.

Made in United States
North Haven, CT
07 May 2025

68654621R00153